COBWEB

Books by Michael Morpurgo include:

ALONE ON A WIDE WIDE SEA
THE AMAZING STORY OF ADOLPHUS TIPS
BILLY THE KID
BORN TO RUN
BOY GIANT
THE BUTTERFLY LION
COOL!
THE DANCING BEAR
DEAR OLLY
AN EAGLE IN THE SNOW
AN ELEPHANT IN THE GARDEN
FARM BOY
FLAMINGO BOY
THE FOX AND THE GHOST KING
KASPAR – PRINCE OF CATS
LISTEN TO THE MOON
LITTLE MANFRED
OUTLAW
RUNNING WILD
SHADOW
SPARROW
TORO! TORO!
WHEN FISHES FLEW

Illustrated in full colour:
THE BOY WHO WOULD BE KING
PINOCCHIO
TALES FROM SHAKESPEARE
THERE ONCE IS A QUEEN
TOTO

For Nick and Helen,

*Remembering your Drovers' Way walk, 250 miles,
from Treginnis in Pembrokeshire to London, in
support of Farms for City Children, and to thank you
for all your help with this book. Cobweb and I could
never have done it without you!*

First published in the United Kingdom by
HarperCollins *Children's Books* in 2024
HarperCollins *Children's Books* is a division of HarperCollins*Publishers* Ltd
1 London Bridge Street
London SE1 9GF

www.harpercollins.co.uk

HarperCollins*Publishers*
Macken House, 39/40 Mayor Street Upper
Dublin 1, D01 C9W8, Ireland

1

ISBN 978–0–00–835213–4

Michael Morpurgo and Michael Foreman assert the moral right to be
identified as the author and illustrator of the work respectively.
A CIP catalogue record for this title is available from the British Library.

Typeset in Aldus LT Std 12/18pt
Printed and bound in the UK using 100% renewable electricity at
CPI Group (UK) Ltd

MICHAEL MORPURGO

COBWEB

Illustrations by Michael Foreman

HARPERCOLLINS
CHILDREN'S BOOKS

CHAPTER ONE

They call me Cobweb. And I know why. I'll tell you why later. I may be a dog, but I know and understand a lot more than people think I do. It's true that I didn't know much and I didn't see much when I was first born, not for a while anyway. I had to learn, like you did. The world was just a foggy, foggy blur to me – a haze of light and shadow and sound and silence, a world of warm milk and closeness and licking and warmth.

I came to know people at first by listening to their voices – and to one voice in particular. The first voice I ever heard. Gentle and soft, it was, as I was picked up and held, cuddled and stroked. The voice said to me: 'Hello, littlest one. I'm Bethan. And I'll look after you always, always. Promise.'

Then came the day when my eyes opened and I saw the world as it is, not blurry at all any more, but clear and bright, just as it has been all my life and every day since. That same day I saw my Bethan for the first time – a face of smiles and laughter. But then, soon enough,

I saw the face of another voice that I had come to know too, a louder voice. This face was hardly ever a smiley one like Bethan's. 'Tad', she called him.

'Don't you mind Tad,' Bethan would say to me. 'He's my father. He can be a bit grumpy these days. He says it's because he's got aching bones, but I know better. He's been like it since . . . since it happened. He's sad. I've been sad too, but you make me happy again.'

Bethan was the one I loved best in the whole world right from the start, because I could tell she loved me best. That's the way love often works, if you didn't know. My mother loved me too, of course, but she had six others like me to feed and look after, so she had to spread her love seven ways. Not easy. She licked me clean, fussed over me and fed me, like she fed all of my six brothers and sisters.

We all of us had to learn to fend for ourselves when it came to feeding – and that wasn't easy for me, being the smallest. I always had to push and wriggle my way through the jumble and tumble of the others, each of us struggling to get to the best feeding place at the front, and all of them fighting to shove me out of the way, topple me out, push me to the back if they could. Mostly, they couldn't. I may have been the smallest, but I was as good a barger as any of them. I had to be.

Anyway, very soon I knew that it was Bethan who really looked after me – really loved me best. She was out working on the farm with Tad most of the time, but whenever she could she'd come into the barn to see me. She would pick me up, carry me about, talk to me, stroke me, kiss my nose. She never wanted to be without me. And I never wanted to be without her. I think she could tell that I needed more looking after than my brothers and sisters, being the smallest, which of course I was. And I liked that.

Soon Bethan was taking me off to all her favourite places on the farm – sometimes even into the farmhouse where she lived with Tad, where she knew, and where I soon discovered, that dogs weren't allowed. Tad kept telling her again and again that farm dogs belonged out in the barn or on the farm.

Bethan told him straight. 'If I can't bring Cobweb inside, Tad, then I'll go and live with him in the barn! Honest I will!' And she meant it too. I could tell. Tad could tell too, so he gave in. He usually gave in. She had a way with him.

After that, Bethan took me in and out of the

farmhouse all she liked. Snug it was in there, on her bed, and warm and lovely. But for a while I still slept at nights with my mother and in amongst all my wriggling brothers and sisters in our corner of the barn. That was snug enough too, and smelly. I was happy with smelly. I'm a dog, remember? So I had the best of both worlds – barn and farmhouse. I was a happy little dog wherever I was, but I was always happiest with Bethan.

Bethan and I, we always understood each other somehow, right from the start. I often knew what she was thinking before she said it, and she always knew what I was thinking before I barked it.

I soon discovered that Bethan had a favourite place she loved to be. Treasure Island.

'I'll take you there one day. There's no treasure,' she told me. 'It's just an old story – an old fairy tale about some treasure chest buried on the island somewhere, full of gold coins – from the wreck of a Spanish galleon. That's what Mami used to tell us.'

Bethan told me her joys and, in time, her sadnesses too. One day she told me of the greatest sadness inside her. I hadn't known the reason, but I had sensed it was in her long before she told me of it.

'Mami's dead, you know. I miss her every day. And I miss Dylan too – my big brother, he was. Best brother anyone could have. And Mami was the best mami too. Tad misses them both every day, every night, like I do. I've never spoken about them out loud to him, nor to anyone else. Only to you.

'Tad doesn't like me to speak their names. He doesn't want to remember them as they were.

But I do. Mami used to tell Dylan and me lots of stories, but her story about the treasure chest hidden away on Treasure Island was my favourite. It was Dylan's favourite too. He always said he was going to find the treasure one day and dig it up, and then we wouldn't have to be poor any more. Do you know what else Mami told us, Cobweb? Mami always said if you believe hard enough in a

story, then it will come true. It's not true – I know that. But I can hope, can't I, Cobweb?

'I hope every day that Mami will come back, but she hasn't, and she won't. And nor has Dylan. Doesn't stop me hoping.

'It happened when I was little. They went out to pick up the lobster pots in the boat one day – five years, three months and two weeks

ago it was – and they just didn't come back. *On the next tide*, I'm always hoping, always telling myself. *They'll come back on the next tide*. But they never do – of course they don't, and I know they never will. Oh, wouldn't it be grand if all we hoped for came true?

'When Tad's deep in his sadness, Cobweb, he goes on and on about how poor we are, about how now that Dylan's gone and Mami is gone, we have to do all the work on the farm and in the house on our own now. We did have Barri to help for a while, from the village, but he wasn't much use, and paying him wasn't worth it, Tad said. And Barri kept telling me it was too much like hard work on the farm. Grumbling all the time, he was. And I didn't like Barri about the place, anyway. He shouted at my sheep and frightened them silly. So, if I'm honest, I'm glad he didn't stay.'

Bethan loved to talk. I didn't understand the half of it, of course, but I loved it when she spoke to me. I felt she was confiding in me, trusting me.

'Barri left to be a soldier, you know,' she said, 'to fight the Frenchies in the war, against Boney. The Frenchies don't have a king like we do, Cobweb. They have an emperor instead. I don't know why. Napoleon, he is – Boney, we call him. And Boney wants to invade us, and we don't want him to, do we? So we're fighting him and he's fighting us. A few young fellows from around here have gone to the war, like Barri did. And we haven't heard of him or seen him since. There's been one or two killed. That's what happens in wars, Cobweb. People die, and that's really sad.

'Anyway . . .' She still hadn't finished. 'Anyway,

Tad and me, we're on our own again now. But the trouble is there aren't enough hours in the day to get all the work done, not enough hands to do it, and stone walls are falling down. A shed blew away in the last gale, and the roof's falling off the house, and there's more gales to come – there always are. And Tad says we'll never have enough money to mend everything, no matter how hard we work on the farm. And he goes on and on about how he knows that there is treasure out there somewhere on Treasure Island, that there must be, and that one day he'll find it and then we'll be rich, and everything will be fine.

'I can't tell him that there's no point in hoping for the impossible, can I? There is no treasure, and Mami and Dylan are gone – gone for good – and we can't bring them back. There's only sheep over there on Treasure Island. My little treasures they are, my lovelies. Treasure enough for me. And there's rabbits over there, of course, Cobweb – lots of rats and rabbits. You'll love the rats and the rabbits. Plenty for you to chase.'

Even when I was a very young pup Bethan would take me with her over in the boat to Treasure Island – to meet the sheep, she said, so I'd get to know them and they'd get to know me. Tad would take my brothers and sisters sometimes, but Bethan only ever took me. I wasn't sure what for to begin with. I was soon to find out.

Chapter Two

Treasure Island might have been a boat ride across the sea, but I soon came to understand it was still a part of the farm – that it was where all the sheep and lambs lived most of the time. When the sea was calm enough, Bethan and Tad would take me across to the island in the rowing boat to see if the sheep were doing well over there.

That was when I first began to discover what my job in life was to be. I hardly had to be told. Somehow, I think I knew already. Tad would whistle and bellow at me, and wave his stick, but

I just seemed to know what to do anyway. I knew I was made for it. Don't ask me how. I would get behind the sheep and let my eye and my bark move them along, gather them together or drive

them on, so Bethan and Tad could see if any of them weren't looking right when they ran – you know, limping a bit. Then I'd herd them into a corner, bunch them all up tight together and lie down, head on my paws, eyeing them. My eyes were enough – with a bark or two from time to time to remind them who was boss. Tad and Bethan would walk in amongst them, able now they were bunched tight to catch any that might not be too well. They'd pick out those that were looking poorly or coughing, and make them better if they could.

Sometimes they'd even bring one of them back in the boat with us if it needed more looking after. Tad could be quite rough with the sheep as he grabbed them by the leg or by the neck, but Bethan was always gentle with them. She'd talk to them to calm them. She loved her 'lovelies' – I could see that. But not as much as she loved me. I could see that too.

It was on Treasure Island where I chased my first rabbit and my first rat, and where I learnt never to chase sheep, but just to let them know I was there, how to move them on without frightening them. Bethan was the best teacher a dog ever had. She was never angry with me, never shouted like Tad did. And Bethan always had a pat or a cuddle for me when I'd done well. So I always did my best. I just wanted her to be proud of me.

I remember well enough the day of the promise. It was a fine day – blue sky, blue sea, flat calm. We had gone off, all three of us, in the boat to Treasure Island to see to the sheep again. We'd had the best of days over there. Tad hadn't

bellowed at me once all day. I'd chased lots of rabbits, and caught a few rats too, which I loved to do. Even Tad gave me a pat for that. He didn't like rats. 'Only good rat's a dead rat,' he'd say.

It happened soon after we'd come home that day. Home for me was always the farmhouse now – my early life in the barn, growing up with all my brothers and sisters, was behind me. Bethan was crouching down beside me in the kitchen as I was drinking from a water bowl. Tad was sitting in his chair by the fire, fast asleep, tired out.

She whispered. 'I was so proud of you today, out there on Treasure Island. And so was Tad. I could see. So now's the moment. You can finish your drink later.' She picked me up and kissed me on the nose. 'Wish me luck, Cobweb,' she said, and she carried me over to where Tad was sitting by the fire.

'Tad,' she said loudly, standing right over him and shaking his shoulder, gently but insistently, to wake him up. 'Tad! It's me. Bethan. Wake up,

Tad.' She went on shaking him until he opened his eyes. When he did, I could see he just wanted to close them again. 'Just to say, Tad, that Cobweb's mine,' Bethan went on. 'He's mine, right? You can have all the other puppies to sell, when the time comes, but Cobweb's mine, right? Promise?'

Tad was cross at being woken, and grumpy. 'What do you want him for? He's just a scrap of a thing – smallest of the lot of them. No, no. We'll sell him on with the others. We need the money. How many times do I have to tell you? We won't have the farm no more without money. Need every penny we can get, and we'll get a fair price for him. He's going to make a good drover's dog, that one. There's a drover I know in town. Like as not, he'll pay good money for him. You've done well with him, Bethan, trained him up well. That dog is good with the sheep, grant you that. But he's a dog, Bethan, that's all – not a friend. Don't you go being silly now. Off you go and leave me be. Can't you see I'm sleeping?'

Now Bethan was as cross as he was. 'I'm not being silly, Tad,' she said. 'And you're not sleeping. And Cobweb is my friend, my best friend. I like him and he likes me. Other children have friends. I don't because we live on the farm, a long way away from the other people in the town. Other children have mothers. And brothers too. I don't because they both died. So I get lonely sometimes, see? And I need a friend. Cobweb's my friend. And, like you said, he's good with the sheep too, best I've ever seen. So I want to have him for my own. You've got to promise. If Mami and Dylan were here, they'd tell you—'

'Don't you dare speak their names! You hear me, Bethan?' Tad's voice was full of tears. 'She shouldn't have gone out fishing in the boat that day. I told her. And all for a lousy lobster or two. But they didn't listen, neither of them. "Oh no, Tad," Dylan says, "Mami and me, we'll be fine." What were they thinking? Why? Why did they go? I told them the sea was too rough. I told them.' Tad was up out of his chair now, and shouting at Bethan, at us both. 'All right, if you want that dog so bad, then you have him – see if I care. Now leave me alone, will you! And don't you ever speak of them again, Bethan, you hear me? Never, never.'

Bethan was as upset as Tad was. She picked me up and was hugging me very tight as she ran out into the farmyard, scattering the hens everywhere as she went. 'Mine, Cobweb, you're mine! And I'm yours.' She was crying, burying her face in my neck. 'But it's true what Tad says. He did tell them – I heard him say there was a wicked west wind coming in, and not to go out in the boat, that he could feel it in the air. He told them it was too choppy in the channel. But Mami went off with Dylan and I never saw them again. But I got you now. You and me, together forever.'

Chapter Three

I promised that I'd tell you how I came to be called Cobweb. Well, I'll tell you now. It's a good story. I like a good story.

I always loved snuffling around in the spidery corners of the barn where I was born – there were always wonderful smells to explore, mouse smell, rat smell, all sorts – and so I'd often come away with cobwebs all over my nose and face. Bethan squealed with laughter every time she saw me covered in cobwebs. I always loved to hear her laugh. And one day when she was brushing the cobwebs off me yet again, she held me up, kissed me on my nose and called me 'Cobweb'. I've been Cobweb ever since. Funny name, but I like it. I'm used to it, I suppose.

So now that you know the story of my early beginnings, and the story of my name, I'm going to tell you the story of the rest of my life – of all of my lives and adventures up till now. And I've had a few, as you are about to find out. And if you find some of them difficult to believe, I'm telling you, I was there!

The truth is I nearly didn't have any more lives at all. It was mostly Tad's fault, but in a way it was my fault too.

Tad was always leaving the door of the farmhouse open. If ever I saw an open door, I'd be through it and gone. I knew there was an exciting new world waiting to be discovered on my own out there, outside the farmhouse. I'd seen something of it already with Bethan, but I wanted to explore more of it. So I escaped and ran off whenever I could.

Every time – and sooner rather than later – Bethan would come looking for me. She'd find me playing with my family in the barn – those of my brothers and sisters that Tad hadn't sold off already – or snuffling around somewhere in the farmyard, or nose to nose with a pig, or rounding up the geese. She'd pick me up, bring me home and tell me not to do it again – to stay home and only go out on the farm with her, that I could get into real trouble out there all on my own, that it was dangerous. Every time I knew she was just pretending to be cross with me. She was protecting me. Bethan was never angry with me – well, almost never.

Anyway, one morning I woke up and saw Tad putting on his boots and going out to work, leaving the door wide open, again. I couldn't resist it, again. Once he was out of the way, I was out of the door in a flash and away. I ventured further that morning than I had ever gone before. Bethan didn't come after me. I was out there, running free, and on my own. There was a wild, blustery wind blowing in, and I loved that. It made me feel

wild too. I was all excited, barking and barking –
at the wind, at the crows, at the whole wonderful
world about me. I was having the time of my life.

I had followed, as usual, where my nose had
led me, across the farmyard, under the gate,
and then for the first time out into the big wide
thistly field beyond. There weren't just prickly
thistles in that field. There were cows in there,
big black cows with horns –
cows that took one
look at me and
charged. They had
eyes that told me
they didn't like
me. They were fast,
but not as fast as me.

I was used to

the sheep on Treasure Island, not these huge horned monsters. I was terrified. I ran as fast as my little legs would carry me, and then squeezed myself, only just in time, under the gate and I was away and out of that field. I stood on the other side and barked back at them triumphantly through the gate. All they could do was stand there, steaming with anger, and moo at me.

In the next field I came to, there were rooks, crowds of rooks, that cawed noisily, raucously at me when they saw me, lots and lots of them, but they were small, so I could chase them. Chasing and smelling, I loved them both as much as each other. Chasing those rooks was as good as chasing the rabbits or rats on Treasure Island.

I was busy chasing them into the far corner of the field, still barking at the wind, when I began to hear a strange and distant sound. It wasn't the crashing rumbling of the waves, which was becoming ever louder and louder as I came closer. I knew the sound of the sea well enough by now. No, this was more like a moaning, a wailing, that seemed to be calling me. It was a sound full of sadness.

I'm a very curious sort of a dog. I always have to find out what I don't know. It's got me into all kinds of difficulties over the years, as you will discover, but that's how I am. I followed my ears now, under the fence and out of the field. Down the winding track through the bracken I went, down and down, until I came round a bend, and there it was, the wide, wide sea, as far as the eye could see, but never as I'd seen it before.

There were huge thundering waves rolling

in, pounding against the cliffs. The beaches and rocks below me were covered in thick white surf. I'd never seen the sea like this before. Above me there were clouds of circling white birds, soaring up there on the wind, crying out loud, diving on me, screeching at me. I knew gulls before from our days on Treasure Island with Bethan and Tad, but only in ones or twos. Now there were hundreds of them, wheeling over my head, diving down so close that sometimes I could feel the wind of their wings. They were coming for me, attacking me, and I was all alone. I had no Bethan to drive them away, to protect me.

I was frightened silly, that's for sure. But I wasn't going to show it. I ran down the track and out on to the beach, barking up at them, telling them I was here, that this was my beach as much

44

as theirs, that I was Cobweb. This usually made
rabbits and rats run away. But these gulls didn't
run away. Down they came again, and again,
screeching and swooping so close that some of
them were nipping the top of my head.

It was me that ran then. I ran hard, as fast as I could through the surf, until I found a way up off the beach and in amongst the rocks. A perfect hiding place, I thought. I crawled in and hid there where they couldn't get at me, still barking my defiance at them. But the gulls didn't go away. They hovered overhead or just sat there on the rocks, eyeing me, waiting for me to come out so they could chase me again. I decided the safest thing to do was to stay where I was till they went away.

I was so tired by this time, covered in foam from the surf, and wet through. I was cold and I was as miserable as I'd ever been. I just wanted to go home to Bethan. But every time I peered out of my hideaway in the rocks the gulls were still there, watching me, waiting for me to come out and make a run for it. All I had to do was wait longer than they did. Exhausted, I closed my eyes, and was asleep before I knew it.

When I woke up, I saw at once that I was in trouble. The waves were crashing in higher, washing in amongst the rocks, flooding into my hideaway. There was water all around me. There was no way now that I could get down to the beach and reach the track back up to the farm and to Bethan. The sea had cut me off. But at least the gulls had all gone. I crawled out of my hiding place. All the time, the waves seemed to be coming in higher, ever closer to me. I couldn't go down and I couldn't stay where I was. I scrambled up over the rocks and up the cliff face as high as I could go, until I found myself on a ledge, unable to climb any further.

That was when I heard that strange moaning, wailing sound again, from somewhere just below me on the rocks.

I saw then that it was a seal. I'd seen them swimming in the sea off Treasure Island. Bethan loved them, and had told me all about them. But I'd never heard one before. Tad hated them because they sometimes pulled his lobster pots to pieces and ate his lobsters. This seal below me had seen me now. He kept looking up at me nervously, and then with the next wave he slipped into the sea and was gone, and I was alone.

There I sat, trembling with cold now, and calling for help, whining, yelping, crying, the waves crashing in against the cliff, each one higher, each one trying to wash me off my ledge. I knew that sooner or later one of them would succeed, and there was nothing I could do about it. I had to keep calling for Bethan. She was my only hope.

Darkness was falling and still the wild waves thundered in. By now I was losing all hope. Shivering, I curled myself tight into a ball into a cleft in the cliff face to try to keep as safe and warm as I could. Soon I felt myself falling into a deep sleep – a warm sleep full of dreams.

And then, out of these dreams, I heard a voice calling me. Bethan! The best voice in the world. And I knew then it wasn't a dream. It was too real. It was my Bethan – I was sure of it. I barked, I whined, I yelped. She called back, her voice closer to me now.

Then I saw her climbing up the rocks towards me, scrambling on her hands and knees, the waves crashing around her. She didn't care about the waves – she just went on climbing – and finally she reached me where I was on my ledge. Bethan grabbed me, held me tight, sat there for a few moments catching her breath. Then she was carrying me down over the rocks, through the pounding surf, until she was running over the beach, through the foam, still clutching me to her, then up the cliff path, across the fields and into the farmhouse. She did not stop, not once, until we were in the kitchen in front of the stove and she was rubbing me down.

When she had finished and I was warm all through again, she held my face in her hands, making me look at her, and spoke to me for the first time since she'd found me.

'Cobweb,' she said. 'Don't you ever go off and leave me again. You hear me? Thought I'd lost you forever, I did. Anything happens to you, I'd never forgive you. And it would break my heart. Twice already I've had my heart broken, with Mami and Dylan. Not again, never again. You listening, Cobweb?'

I was listening. I told her so with my eyes, and my tail. And she cried then, burying her head in my neck. She likes a good cry, does my Bethan. I promised myself there and then never to go off on my wandering ways again. She had saved my life, after all, my second life. And, anyway, I loved her, pure and simple. I would never leave her ever again – never do anything to upset her.

But life changes, and things happen. Things you can do nothing about.

CHAPTER FOUR

That day, when Bethan carried me home into the farmyard, I was famous. I was everyone's favourite. My brothers and sisters, those that were still with us, were bounding about me in their excitement. And my mother too was all over me, licking me from head to tail. Even those fearsome black cows standing there mooing at the gate seemed happy to see me.

But, as I was to discover, there was less of a warm welcome from Tad. He was cross with Bethan when she told him where she'd found me, how she'd climbed up and rescued me from the rocks, but he was even more cross with me for wandering off. He said nothing to me, but he kept looking at me all evening over his supper. I could read his thoughts exactly. I could tell that, whereas before he had found me just a bit of a nuisance, now he wanted me gone. I can tell a lot from a look. It turned out I was right too.

He came down early in the morning while it was still dark, while Bethan was still asleep upstairs. His voice was a whisper as he bent down to pick me up. 'You little beggar you,' he hissed. 'You nearly drowned my Bethan yesterday, running off like you did. I've lost two of my family already to the sea. And yesterday you nearly took the last one from me. You're trouble, Cobweb, nothing but trouble, and you got to go, before you do more harm. I made up my mind. You're going to go missing. I'll tell Bethan you've wandered off again. She'll go looking for you, but she won't find you this time, that's for certain sure. When you don't come back, she'll cry buckets for a day or two. But she'll get over it. And she won't ever know where you've gone nor what I've done with you.'

And with that he picked me up by the scruff of my neck, dropped me into a sack and carried me off out of the house. Wherever he was taking me, it was a long walk, with me slung over his shoulder, swinging about in the dark of the sack.

He talked to me from time to time as thoughts came to him, in his gentler voice now.

'You brought this on yourself, Cobweb. I could have drowned you in the pond, or put you in a sack and thrown you in the sea. But I'm not doing that, am I? No, I had a better idea . . . I'm going to sell you at the market in town, to my friend Morgan – Drover Morgan we call him. Morgan's always been after one of my dogs. Likes a good Pembrokeshire corgi, he does. Best droving dog in the whole world, he says. He'll pay good money for you. And I need the money bad, Cobweb, that's the truth of it. No money in farming these days, not with this war going on. You won't make much, but you'll make something. And I need every penny. I'm telling you, every bit counts. Drover Morgan won't know you're good for nothing, always running off like you do. And you can stop your wriggling, Cobweb. No way out of this sack, I promise you. Not far now.'

Tad talked to me, talked to himself, sang and whistled as he went along. Maybe it was the swinging about in the sack and the singing, but somehow I dropped off to sleep. I only woke because there was a new noise all around me – the sound of lots of people like Tad, with rasping voices, talking loudly, laughing raucously. And there were farm smells and sounds all around me, of horses, of pigs, cows, sheep, hens and ducks.

I suddenly found myself lifted roughly by the neck out of the sack and set down on a table. I was surrounded by faces peering down at me, laughing at me – strange fingers opening my mouth, strange hands feeling along my back and my legs and my feet. Tad had his gruff voice again, his arguing voice. He was still holding me fast by the scruff of my neck, holding me up and dangling me in the air to show me off to everyone.

'Five shillings. You can buy him off me for five shillings, Drover Morgan, and not a penny less,' Tad was saying. 'Look at him. Little he may be, but I'm telling you true, Morgan, he's the best dog I've had in years. And everyone knows your old drover dog, your Goodlad, is getting on these days. You've said it yourself often enough. This one's the best there is, Drover. You'll see. Obedient he is too. Never wanders off. First time I saw him, I thought: drover's dog. A proper working drover's dog for my friend Drover Morgan.'

To be honest, I had no idea at the time where

I was or what was going on. I'd never been to a market before, never seen so many people or animals in one place, never heard so much noise. All I understood was that Tad had taken me away from my Bethan, and was trying to get rid of me – to sell me to this Drover Morgan. Right from the start, I did not like the look of this man one bit. He had a face like the biggest rat in our barn, fierce and whiskery, with little eyes. And when he talked to me he had a voice that growled. So I growled back.

And I hated how Tad was holding me tight by the neck like he was. I could hardly breathe. I struggled, but that only made it worse. I yelped and barked all I could, but that only made the people all around laugh at me more. I longed for Bethan, for my family, for my mother – longed to be back in the safety and the quiet of the barn.

And suddenly, like a miracle, there she was. My Bethan. I saw her, right there, pushing her way towards me through the crowd of noisy men, then reaching out and taking me away from Tad. A silence had fallen all around me.

'What's she doing here?' said someone. 'We can't have little girls coming into the market like this.'

Tad stood there speechless, too shocked even to be angry.

My Bethan spoke up then in front of Tad, in front of Drover Morgan, and all these other faces, her voice as calm and quiet as you like, so quiet everyone was suddenly silent all around.

'What she's doing here,' she said, '"this little girl", as you call her, is righting a wrong, that's what. This is my dog. Tad knows he's my dog, my Cobweb. He promised me I could keep him. He's still got two other puppies of his own. Yes, Cobweb runs off, goes on his wanderings, but that's how he is, and that's how I like him. He's a free spirit, like me. Cobweb and me, we're family, like brother and sister we are.

'Tad,' she went on, still clutching me to her, 'I'm taking him home. And don't you try to stop me neither. Or next time I'll run away with him, and for good too, and then you won't have anyone to make your lunch or your tea, will you? No one to help you look after the sheep, to bring in the wood for the fire, no one to feed the hens, no one to darn your socks, or cook your food neither.'

We walked away from the market then, me and Bethan, leaving a stunned silence and all those gaping mouths behind us. I trotted along the cobbled street at her heels, so proud of my brave Bethan, and so relieved to be alone with her once more, and safe. I never wanted to see that rat-face Drover Morgan again.

But sometimes wishes don't come true, and sometimes you get people wrong.

CHAPTER FIVE

So that was twice my Bethan had saved me. She didn't speak to Tad for days after that. She hardly let me out of her sight. She took me with her whenever she went out on the farm, and at nights she took me upstairs with her and I slept with her on her bed. Tad didn't like it, and I could see he was quite grumpy about it. But he was too ashamed to do or say anything.

But he soon got used to it. He didn't like me there, but he put up with me, and I put up with him. He'd scoop me off chairs sometimes, and nudge me aside with his foot if ever I got in his way. I made myself useful, chased out any mice that dared venture into the house. He'd give me a pat sometimes when I did that, and some cheese. He was all right, Tad, when he wasn't being grumpy. But grumpy was how he was, mostly – grumpy and sad.

I'd still play out on the farm with my brothers and sisters sometimes, but then they were soon sold off, and not there any more. My mother was there, of course. These days, with no puppies to look after any more, she was busy out on the farm with Tad, driving his cows and pigs, bringing them inside at night, taking them out in the morning. I watched her at work. I was looking and learning. She was the crow-chaser and rabbit-chaser too. She'd sit up on Buzzard Rock in the middle of the farm, and if ever the crows came down to feed in the cornfield she'd soon chase them off. She was too busy to pay attention to me any more. But I didn't mind. I had my Bethan to look after me. All day and all night now, every day and every night, we were together.

She'd talk to me, sing to me, call me. I learnt all her calling whistles when we were out with the sheep on Treasure Island. I knew when to run out around them, when to lie down, nose to the ground and be still, when to come close to them, when to keep my distance, when to bark at them, what to do when one of them went astray, how to make quite clear who was boss, with a little nip here and a little growl there. I loved my work, because I loved to be with my Bethan and, if I'm honest, I loved the sheep too – loved looking after them as much as Bethan did.

I loved the smells on Treasure Island too. There were different smells over there – more holes freshly dug, by rabbits mostly, more holes to get my snout down. Any spare moment, while they were having something to eat or drink, I'd be digging away. I never found anything much worth eating, but that didn't matter. I loved the sniffing and the searching and the digging. I was never happier.

So we grew up together, Bethan and me, the two of us happy around the barns and the fields, chasing each other through the shallows down on the beaches. My best moments of all were with Bethan up on Buzzard Rock, looking out for crows and chasing them off, showing them who was boss on this farm. Mother would be with us sometimes up on the rock, when she wasn't busy with Tad around the farm. She was very much his dog, and I was Bethan's. But we'd go out running together, digging together, playing together, then come back hot and happy and panting and lie down on Buzzard Rock beside Bethan. My mother and Bethan, they meant the world to me.

It wasn't a happy time entirely, though. Bethan was often upset, not just about missing her Mami and Dylan, but also about the war that was still going with Boney and the Frenchies. She talked of it often – how more of the young men were going off to fight, and more of them were not coming home again. How there were more widows in black in town.

I'd sit there beside her on the cliffs, looking out to sea, her hand resting on my neck for comfort. I knew how to cheer her spirits. So I'd run off down to the beach, and she'd come running after me, calling me to come back. Then we'd be down on the beach and I'd be barking at her to throw stones or sticks for me to chase into the sea, and she was soon laughing away her sadness, and all would be well again.

But then came the day when we had real trouble. The day that woman arrived, and our whole world turned upside down. For Bethan and for me, all the happy days were over.

Bethan told me all about her – told me the whole story. We were up on Buzzard Rock. I'd chased away a few crows and some gulls too, and was sitting there quite happily beside her, still panting and a bit out of breath, when she told me. I knew something was wrong. She'd hardly paid me any attention all morning, not a pat, not a stroke, not a cuddle, and that wasn't like my Bethan at all. Then out it all came, and with tears too.

'Oh, Cobweb,' she said, covering her face with her hands. 'I can't bear it. I can't. Her instead of Mami. I miss Mami something dreadful every day, I do, Cobweb. She was lovely. She was perfect. And now he does *this*, brings in *her* instead of Mami.' She had to stop to wipe away her tears.

Then she told me more. 'Tad comes in yesterday, smiling all over his face, like the cat that's got the cream. And do you know what he says? He says, "I've got good news. You're going to have a new mami, Bethan."

'I told him straight. "I don't want a new Mami," I said.

'"You'll like her," he tells me. "You know that nice man you met a while back, in town that day – Drover? Drover Morgan? Well, she's his cousin, Megan. Married yesterday we were. And you got to be nice to her and respectful. She's moving in here with us tomorrow."'

Bethan could hardly get her words out she was crying so much. 'She's moving in tomorrow, Cobweb. And I don't want her here. It's Mami's house. I got my own mami. She may not be here any more, but she's still my mami, and always will be too. Crying like a baby, I am. Sorry, Cobweb, I don't want to upset you. But I can't help it.'

But very soon she had a whole lot more to cry about, and so did I. Here's what happened.

Megan came to live with us the very next day, as Tad said she would, and she came in a big pink bonnet. Everything about her was big. The moment she stepped inside the house, she filled it. She was loud too. She had a big voice that never stopped talking, great clumsy feet that trod on my paws, more than once.

She was whiskery too, with a ratty face. She was quite like I remembered her cousin – like Drover Morgan, but in a pink bonnet. Tad told Bethan she was to call her Auntie Megan from now on.

When she saw me there in the house, her eyes looked down at me like daggers. 'I don't like dogs in the house,' was the very first thing she said. 'Dogs belong outside. Smelly creatures. Hairy creatures. Out!'

So from the first day she arrived I was put out of the door and I slept in the barn that night. And I slept in the barn every night after that. But I wasn't alone. My mother was with me, and night after night my Bethan came out and slept with us too. I was with her in the yard when she stood there and told Tad straight out that she refused to sleep in the farmhouse unless I was allowed to sleep with her on her bed in her room, as usual. Tad shouted at her, and I've never heard him do that before. And my Bethan just stood there, and shouted back at Tad. And when Auntie Megan heard the shouting and came out to see what was going on, my Bethan told her face to face just what she thought of her. I enjoyed that.

Bethan told me later that she preferred the barn anyway because *she* wasn't there, and because she liked to be with me, and to be with the lambing sheep to keep an eye on them, and because of the barn owl nesting up in the rafters that we both loved to see flying in and out, feeding her hissing owlets.

So we were happy enough in the barn. We had each other, and my mother too, the best of both my worlds. But not for long. Tad and 'Auntie

Megan' both came into the barn together one morning and stood there glaring down at us. Tad did the talking, but he was saying what Megan wanted him to say – I could see that.

'Now, Bethan,' he said. 'We've had quite enough of this. The nights are cold. You'll catch your death sleeping out here. Either you come and sleep in the house and behave yourself or . . .' He looked across at Megan, hesitating. He didn't seem to want to go on. Then he spluttered it out. 'Or that dog has to go.'

'Go where?' Bethan asked.

'Go to live with Drover Morgan like I wanted him to before – your Auntie Megan's cousin. I mean it, Bethan. Go on like this and the dog goes.'

Bethan did not hesitate for one moment. 'She's not my auntie. And if Cobweb goes, Tad, I go,' she told him. 'I mean that. And if she makes Cobweb stay outside, makes him sleep out here in the barn, then I'm sleeping out here with him, all the way through the winter if I have to. I don't mind.'

My Bethan was magnificent in her defiance, in her anger. Tad and Megan, they both stood there looking at one another, flummoxed, neither of them knowing what to say. Then came a surprise. Megan smiled. I think it was the first time I ever saw her smile. And when she spoke now, she was speaking gently, kindly. That wasn't like her, either. Something was wrong. Auntie Megan was pretending. I was sure of it. I can always tell if people are pretending.

'I certainly admire your spirit, young lady,' she said. 'And, of course, your father is quite right: you can't go on sleeping out here, not with these frosty nights. So I've been thinking. You bring the nice little dog in, and you have him up on your bed at nights. I'll get used to it. I was brought up to believe that animals should live outside the house, and people inside. But I can see now how much you and Cobweb like to be together. And he's a sweet enough little dog, as dogs go. So let's all be friends, shall we? No more harsh words. After all's said and done, we're family now, aren't we?'

I could see from the look on Bethan's face that she didn't believe a word Megan had said, and neither did I. But that didn't matter. It was a victory, of sorts. That night I slept inside the warmth of the house again, happily curled up on the end of my Bethan's bed. We had won!

Or, at least, we thought we had.

Chapter Six

Megan was all smiles after that. Tad was happy because she baked the best pies and the best cakes he'd ever tasted. And they were good too. I got to try the leftovers. Even my Bethan grudgingly had to admit that they were delicious.

Spring was coming. The lambs were doing well, the cows were loving the new grass and giving down more milk than ever. Megan was churning the butter, which was turning out as gold as the sun. The hens and the geese were laying. Everyone was happy about the farm. Blue skies, calm seas. Prices were good in the market. All seemed well.

But it wasn't.

I didn't see it coming. And my Bethan didn't see it coming, either. And nor did Tad.

I remember the morning it happened. Bethan was excited. It was round-up day on Treasure Island, she told me, and we'd be going to fetch the sheep back from the island to take some of them to sell at the market. We'd have to pick them out, go back and forth with them in the boat and bring them home to the farm. And I'd be going with her, on my first round-up.

We all went down to the beach together, and there was our boat waiting for us, and lots of our farming neighbours were there too with their boats, helping out. Bethan told me it was always like that when we brought the sheep back from Treasure Island.

Tad was standing in the shallows, ready to push off. Mother was in the boat already, barking for me, calling me. I was waiting on the beach for Bethan to come and pick me up as she always did and carry me to the boat. I always liked working the sheep with her, loved being with her. This was going to be a great day. I was thinking of all the exploring out on the island, all the sniffing I could do, and the digging.

Bethan came running down the beach then, calling for me. But that was when I found myself suddenly scooped up and held. It was Megan. She was holding me tight – very tight, too tight. And it wasn't out of love. I knew something was wrong. I struggled, but there was no escape. She was too strong. Bethan stopped and gave her a look. She knew something was wrong too.

'Come on, Bethan,' Tad called out. 'Haven't got all day, have we?'

Tad was pushing off already, then clambering in over the side and sitting down, taking the oars, getting ready to row. Bethan hesitated for a while, looking at me, looking at Megan, anxiously, angrily. Then she turned away, waded out and climbed reluctantly into the boat with Tad.

'Come along, Megan,' Tad was saying. 'You can give the dog to Bethan. He's better with her in the boat – he gets excited.' He was standing up, holding out his hand. 'I'll help you in, dear.'

'I thought I'd keep Cobweb here with me,' Megan called out, holding me ever tighter, her fingers digging into my neck. 'Cobweb can stay here with me on the beach and when you get back with the sheep he can help drive them up the cliff path to the farm. You've got the other one. And I don't like being alone on the farm. He'll be company, won't you, Cobweb? I'll look after him – don't you worry. We'll get to know each other. Off you go now.' And she turned and walked away.

I could see Tad was surprised. He was frowning. He was upset. He hadn't been expecting this. Bethan was arguing with him, pleading with him. 'Tad! Cobweb, he always comes with us. Always. Tad! Don't let her do it.'

Tad didn't seem to know what to do or say.
In the end he said nothing, but sat down and
just began to row hard out towards the island,

with all the other boats around us. My mother

was barking to me across the water. I knew from

her bark that she was trying to warn me. I barked

back as best I could. I could hear Bethan was crying now, begging Tad to go back for me. And all the while Megan was carrying me away up the beach, gripping me so tight I could hardly breathe, and holding my mouth shut, telling me to be quiet. I was struggling all the while to break free of her. And she was hissing at me, her teeth clenched with fury. 'This'll teach that Bethan girl a lesson. This'll teach you a lesson too. You're never going to see her again, never. You're going to be a drover dog for my cousin Morgan. And Morgan's drover dogs do what they are told. No more cuddles for you, Cobweb. You don't do what he says, you try to escape, and he'll beat you within an inch of your life! No one better with a whip than he is.'

When we reached the farm, there was Drover

Morgan, standing by his horse and cart, waiting for us in the farmyard. He was holding out a corn sack, wide open, and I knew what that meant. I struggled to break free of Megan as she tried to drop me in. I twisted and turned, did all I could to bite her. I tried to bite Drover Morgan when he grabbed me too, but I couldn't. Then I was in the sack, and it was tied up, all daylight suddenly gone. I was swinging about in the dark, and felt myself being dumped in the back of the cart. Soon it was bumping away down the farm track, the whip cracking, the horse snorting.

I barked and I yelped, even though I knew it was no use. My Bethan could not hear me. She was far away across the water, on the island by now. The further the horse and cart took me – and the journey seemed like it was going on forever – the less chance there was that I would ever see her or my mother or my home again. Bethan had rescued me twice before. This time I knew I would have to rescue myself.

CHAPTER SEVEN

All the way I yelped and whined for Bethan in my misery. I had one thought in my mind. Escape. The trouble was that Drover Morgan seemed to know it. From the moment we arrived at his farm, when he lifted me out of the sack, he had me tied up.

I had never before in my life been tied up,

not until now. And I did not like it, not one bit. All day, all night, I'd be tied up. I could only ever run to the end of my rope. I tried again and again running to the end of it to break free. No good. I tried chewing through the rope. No good. Even by the fire in his cottage Drover Morgan still kept me tied up. In the days that followed, wherever I went, in the back of his cart, or out in the fields with all his sheep and cattle – and he had lots of them, many more than we had back home on Bethan's farm – I was always kept tied to the end of a rope. I was never free to run, never free to go off on my wanders. How I missed following my nose, seeing where the scent led me, and the digging whenever I found something. How I missed chasing the crows and gulls. How I missed my freedom. And how I missed Bethan.

But at least I had a friend in Goodlad, Drover Morgan's old dog. Drover Morgan was very proud of Goodlad. You could hear it in his voice whenever he talked about him. And Drover Morgan liked to talk. How he liked to talk.

'He's a collie dog is my Goodlad, old like me, but he still goes like the wind, turns on a penny. Him and me, we work the cattle and sheep together, have done for years. I'm no master, he's no slave. He can drive those sheep and cattle just by looking at them. Like me, he got rickety legs and misty eyes. But he goes on, and so do I. 'Swhy we need you, Cobweb. 'Swhy when my cousin Megan offered you to me, I agreed to take you. Almost bought you once before, if you remember. Got you this time. Young legs, bright eyes. Just what I want. You'll be a big help. Over two hundred and fifty miles to London, and more than two hundred and fifty back, long way – that's where the market is. I've done it dozens of times. And I love it too. It's a good life out on the road – hard life, but it's a good living. You'll love it, Cobweb, once you get used to it. You do what Goodlad does, and everything will be fine. You'll soon learn, and we'll soon be friends. You'll see.'

Already I could see that Goodlad was old and slow, but when he was out working the sheep and cattle that didn't seem to matter. He never had to chase them. They all knew he was there, watching them. His eyes told them everything they needed to know. What he did, I did. It was Goodlad who taught me everything I know about driving. And I had a lot to learn.

Megan turned out to be quite wrong about

Drover Morgan. He may have kept me tied up, but he never beat me, nor whipped me, as she said he would. I realised soon enough she'd only said that to frighten me. Yes, he had a ratty face, and a bit of a growly voice sometimes, but I learnt that you can't judge man or dog or anyone by the look of a face or the sound of a voice or a bark.

He looked after me well. I had a bed box to share with Goodlad by the fire, and Drover Morgan would talk to me more and more as we got to know one another, and not in his growly voice. The time came that he was not tying me up but trusting me not to run off. I stayed with him because I knew I was far from Bethan and had no idea where to run off to, how to find my way home.

I missed her, of course, but Drover Morgan was kind enough. Goodlad had quickly become a good friend to me, a good teacher too. I was being well looked after. I knew that if I went home, even if I could find it, Megan would still be there and would find another way to get rid of me.

I decided to stay where I was, become a drover's dog, and see where life led me. It would be an adventure – I was sure of that.

Then one evening by the fire Drover Morgan started talking to me, confiding in me gently, like a friend – more like Bethan had, and Tad sometimes too.

'Truth be told, Cobweb, I don't much like Cousin Megan. I know I should, her being my cousin and all. Bossy she is, terrible bossy. And greedy too. Your poor Tad will soon find that out, your Bethan too, if they haven't already. She's got a nasty streak in her. Not much to like in her. Can't think what Tad was doing marrying her. No one can. Lonely, I expect, after that accident. Terrible loss for him it was. Terrible.

'I been alone all my life. So I don't miss no one. I'm happy in the house just with you, Cobweb, and Goodlad. Goodlad likes you. Truth be told, I like you, Cobweb. But I can't expect you to like me, can I? Not after I took you away like I did, and tying you up. I only did it so you didn't run back to Bethan. I knew you would, see. Because you love her, right? And when I untied you, you stayed. Had to take the risk sometime that you'd stay. And I'm glad, really glad, you did. So's Goodlad.

'Listen, Cobweb. I got more truth to tell you. Truth is I need you, need you bad. You're going to make a fine drover dog. Goodlad won't mind me saying it – he's like me, getting on in years. Not what he was. Happens when you're old. He's not good on his legs no more, bit like me, and he don't see or hear as well as he did. Bit like me too. The thing is, I got fifty or more cattle and over three hundred sheep to drive up to London. You're brave with the cattle – I've seen you – and good with the sheep. I need the help. That's why I took you on. And Goodlad needs the help. He's taken to you – I can see he has. But I got to be able to trust you, Cobweb. You got to be good, and not run away. You listening to me, Cobweb? You promise and I'll never tie you up again. And what's more, when we get back, if you like,

I'll take you home to Bethan. That's a promise. Promise me now?'

I promised with my eyes. At least if I was free to run and work, I'd be half free. I'd be happy enough. Anyway, he'd promised to take me home to Bethan. I was more than happy with that, for the moment. And, if truth be told, I had made a new friend in Goodlad, and the longer I was with Drover Morgan, the more I liked him. Not as much as Bethan, of course. But he was kind. He fed me, looked after me. I felt safe with him. I'd find my way back to Bethan one day – I was sure of that – but for the moment I'd stay with Drover Morgan and Goodlad, become a drover's dog and hope for the best. What else could I do?

CHAPTER EIGHT

I soon found out that working as a drover's dog was different altogether from being a farm dog back on Bethan's farm by the sea. Every day, farmers from all around were bringing more cattle and sheep on to Drover Morgan's land, and every one of these animals was a stranger to Goodlad and me. It's not at all easy when you don't know them, and when they don't know you. We herded them as best we could into different fields and pens that were strange to them, that made them jittery. And we made them nervous too.

We soon found out the difficult ones, soon picked out the leaders. Every herd of cattle, every flock of sheep has a leader. Often more than one, I was discovering. I could see what Goodlad was up to.

He'd make sure the leader knew that he was in charge, not by frightening them, but by getting to know every one of them, treating each differently, persuading them, with a bark when necessary, with a threat of a nip on the leg if they were being obstinate. Persuade the leader and you persuade them all.

But that persuasion was mostly with eyes. Goodlad would lie down flat on the grass, his head lowered on to his paws, his eyes fixed on one and on all of them at the same time – which is quite a trick – and let those eyes do the barking and nipping. I learnt his tricks fast. I did the same. And it worked. Under his tuition, I very soon became a drover dog, and we became a team, just the two of us herding the animals into a new field with fresh grass, or into the barn, where Drover Morgan would check them over, their feet especially. It was going to be the longest walk of their lives, he told us, so they needed to be walking on strong, healthy feet. Farriers came on to the farm to shoe the cows, so there was a lot of smoke about as they burnt iron shoes on to their feet, and a lot of angry cows afterwards. They didn't like it one bit, and I don't blame them.

Out in the fields, as we drove the animals, Drover Morgan would always be up on his horse, looking on. He hardly had to whistle or call out. Goodlad could read his mind – they knew one another so well. That trick took longer for me to learn, but I was learning, fast, and enjoying it too.

Every day brought more animals to Drover

Morgan's land. He was becoming busier and busier, impatient, and he'd tell us why. He told us everything, which was good because all this was new to me. From up on his horse, he'd tell us his hopes and worries.

'We're droving a hundred and twenty cattle and three hundred and fifty sheep all the way to London – two hundred and fifty miles aways. And there's some not here, and they should be here. I've only got enough grass in my fields for another two days at the most. Farmer Jones from Solva is late again with his cattle. He's always late. So is that David Williams from St David's. Bring them by yesterday. That's what I tell them every year. You want your animals to get to market in London? You want me to take them there? You want your money? Then bring me your animals now. I need them now – by yesterday would be better – or I'll go without them. I wouldn't, of course, and they know it, that's the trouble.

'But I'm worried. It's the weather, see? The weather's set fair at the moment. You can see it in the clouds, feel it in the wind. I have to get these animals over the mountains before the rain comes. You don't want to cross those mountains with the tracks turned to mud. Once we're over the mountains and down in Golden Valley we'll be all right – it's more sheltered down there, see. You know that, Goodlad, don't you? You've been there often enough. Nightmare the mountain is in nasty weather. Worried sick, I am. And then everyone you talk to is worried about that Napoleon coming over and invading us. Boney, we call him. You've heard of him, have you? French Emperor. Doesn't like us and we don't like him. Been at war with him for years, we have. Doesn't know when he's beaten – that's his trouble. He'll always come back and have another go.

'But I'm not that worried about Boney – no, not one bit. All I want is Farmer Jones and David Williams to get their sheep and cattle over here with the others, and then we can all be on our way and off to London before the rain comes. I'm going to ride over and give them a piece of my mind. You stay here and look after things. All right?'

And he was gone, leaving us to guard all the cattle and all the sheep. Of course, we dogs are not good with numbers. We don't do counting. Truth is, we don't need to. Goodlad taught me this trick too. We look a flock of sheep over, wander around a herd of cattle, and we just know if they're all there or not. We don't need to count.

It's the sheep that go missing mostly. They roll over on to their backs by a hedge somewhere, and can't get back up again. They lie there kicking their legs, struggling to get up. Leave them there too long and the crows will come down and start pecking. And that will be the end of them. So we've got to keep a sharp lookout.

All was well by the next day. No sheep on their backs. David Williams brought his sheep over in the morning, and Farmer Jones came that afternoon with his cattle. Drover Morgan was chuckling into his glass of beer by the fire that evening. We lay at his feet in our bed box,

Goodlad and me, half awake, half listening to him.

'Early morning start, boys. I want to be on the road by first light. You make the best of this fire and have a good sleep. We'll have a hearty breakfast together, then off we go to London. You haven't been to London before, have you, Cobweb? People. You've never seen nothing like them. People all over, like ants they are. And the buildings, high as the sky. Some of them make St David's Cathedral look like a shed. Honest they do. My first time there, I never knew there could be so many people in all the world. All I can say is you'll be pleased to come home again. Sleep now, there's good boys.'

And he left us there, Goodlad and me, by the fire. Goodlad was asleep in a moment. I wasn't. I knew I was about to set out on a great adventure, see places and people I'd never seen before. I couldn't sleep a wink, not until I thought of Bethan. Thoughts of her covered me like a warm blanket, and soon I was away with her in my dreams.

CHAPTER NINE

I was thinking of Bethan again when the sun came up over the hill the next morning as we were setting off. It was something Drover Morgan said as he was leading the way up on his horse, leading the sheep on. 'Come along, my lovelies,' he said. 'Come along now.'

I'd be following on after the sheep, but more

than following on, keeping them going, my eye on the stragglers, my occasional bark reminding them I was there, that I meant business. All I had to do was to pretend I was Goodlad, pretend I was bigger than I was and braver, with a louder bark and sharper teeth, and that I knew what I was doing. That's what Drover Morgan had told me, that's what Goodlad had showed me and that's what I did.

From time to time, I'd keep looking over my shoulder at the herd of cattle that trudged along after me, their tongues licking their noses, their tails whisking. Some stopped to pull at the grass on the verges as we passed, tearing at it, chewing on it, as they went. There was a constant murmur of bleating of sheep in front of me, of lowing cattle behind. Occasionally I heard Goodlad right at the back, his bark urging the cattle on.

Down into the valleys we went, through villages where the children waved from windows, and some came rushing out of their houses to greet us. Everyone seemed to know Drover Morgan. He was much liked, and famous, I was to learn, wherever we travelled. Over rushing streams we went, across bridges and then uphill towards the cloud-covered mountains ahead. We'd stop to rest from time to time on a village green, or on a meadow down by a river. My feet and my legs always needed a rest, I can tell you. But even when we were resting Goodlad and I had to keep an eye out, to be sure none of the animals strayed.

If they were grazing, and left in peace, they were settled and happy enough. But Drover

Morgan had warned me often to be on my guard night and day against local dogs – farm dogs, village dogs, wild dogs or foxes – anything that might frighten the sheep and stampede the cattle. So like Goodlad, whenever we stopped to rest, I kept my back to our animals, and my eye and my nose out for any wandering farm dogs or foxes.

I watched Goodlad all I could. I studied him. At the sight of any dog, his hackles would go up, he'd bare his teeth and there'd be a growling like thunder from deep inside him. Then he'd set off, not running at them, but stalking, head lowered, pointing at them, every step towards them a threat. I saw it worked – worked every time. So I did the same. I became so fierce sometimes that I almost frightened myself. And always the local dogs backed off, just like that. I did wonder what might happen one day if they didn't, if I had to fight. I'd never been in a fight in my life, just play fights, fun fights, back on Bethan's farm, with my brothers and sisters.

Worse still, Drover Morgan had warned me, were cattle thieves, the sheep stealers. Highwaymen, all of them on the lookout for droving herds just like ours. 'They'll like as not have dogs with them, Cobweb,' said Drover Morgan. 'But you stand your ground, make like you're a wolf and look fierce, till I come. One look at my musket will soon see them off. You got to remember, Cobweb, they're just as frightened as we are. All we have to do is look them in the eye and growl better than they do. A couple of good growlers like you two, and an angry old drover with a wicked-looking musket – they'll run. You'll see.'

Because Goodlad was wary, I was too, of thieves and dogs. A few dogs tried to bother us, but we soon saw them off. Foxes would come prowling around the sheep at nights, but Goodlad and I soon chased them away. Nights we would spend in a field close to an inn. There was usually a stream or river running by, so there was water enough for the cattle and sheep, and us.

Drover Morgan would sleep and eat at the inn, but before he went in he always made sure we had something to eat, and somewhere we could sleep out of the rain – a shed or a barn. Every place we stopped was alive with new smells. Sometimes I just wanted to go off and follow my nose. But I couldn't. I had my work to do, and I didn't want to let Goodlad down.

The innkeepers all knew Drover Morgan and

Goodlad – like family almost. It was obvious by now to me that Drover Morgan must have come this same way, stopped in the same inns, every time. He seemed to have friends wherever we stopped for the night. They seemed to like me too, especially the children, who made a great fuss of me, and I liked that, so long as they didn't touch my ears. I don't like that. Like Goodlad and Drover Morgan, I was made to feel at home wherever we stopped. But we never stayed more than one night. It was up at dawn every day, and off.

Whilst the weather was good, it was all fine. Drover Morgan kept a gentle pace ahead of us on his horse, and rested us often enough so we could keep going. But already a few of the sheep and cows were walking lame, despite their iron shoes – especially when we came to the steep, rocky tracks over the mountains. They'd slip and stumble on their hooves. Our paws were better, but too soft. I had to tread carefully, picking my way along the rock-strewn paths.

And with the mountains came the driving rain and the wild wind and the sinking mud. Now Goodlad and I had to work much harder to keep the animals going. Some were really struggling up the slopes, often losing their footing, slipping to their knees and finding it hard to get up. Drover Morgan had to dismount to help them.

'Not far now, boys,' he would shout to us through the wind and the hail.

Oh, it *was* far, very far – very wet and very cold. But we kept going. The animals kept going. We had no choice.

And then at long last we were over the top of
the mountain, and going down into the shelter of
the valleys again, and after a while there ahead
was an inn, with smiling faces to welcome us,

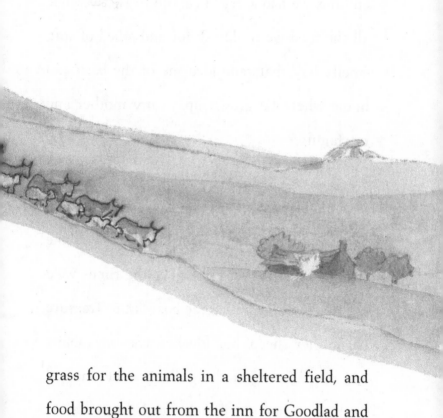

grass for the animals in a sheltered field, and
food brought out from the inn for Goodlad and
me, a warm fire and a meal for Drover Morgan
and a stable for his exhausted horse. He brought

a bowl of his leftovers for us, and told us we were the best drover dogs in the world. Goodlad and me, we had a dry shed, out of the weather, all the food we could ask for and a bed of soft, smelly hay that reminded me of the barn and home where I'd grown up, of my mother and my family.

And whenever my thoughts turned to home, I would daydream of my days with Bethan, her gentle voice, the touch of her hand as she stroked me. I would remember the times we'd had down on the beach, the boat out to Treasure Island, her sheep, her lovelies, chasing rabbits and rats, barking at the gulls. It made me sad to think of her, but I could not help myself. It was where my mind went to whenever I was not too busy droving. And every time the sadness of missing her came over me I was comforted by the promise that Drover Morgan had made me that I could go back to her after my droving work was over. That thought kept me going no matter how tired and cold I was, how homesick I felt for Bethan.

It was easy to sleep, easy to dream, but I had to keep an eye out, an ear too. And my hearing, I had noticed, was sharper than Goodlad's. I realised that my eyes were sharper too. I knew more and more as the days passed that he was relying on me to be his eyes and ears, that he wasn't just teaching me to be a drover's dog, but really needed my help, that we were doing this together. In just a short time, under his guidance and friendship, I grew up. I was learning the ways of the world and finding my place in it, and my place was at Goodlad's side.

But when I did have my turn to sleep, how I slept.

CHAPTER TEN

No day was like another on our journey. No village we passed through, no town, no inn, no path or track was like any other. And the people were different too, everywhere we went. Some were wary of us, I could see that, and just wanted our animals to be gone through their village as soon as possible. Most people were more than pleased to welcome Drover Morgan and Goodlad again as we passed through. And the children often made a great fuss of me, which I liked a lot.

But there were times when villagers scowled at us as we passed by – some even shouted at us and threw stones. When that happened, Goodlad ignored it, so I did too. I knew why. We had the animals to look after. We had to move them on, keep them calm. Once or twice, Drover Morgan rode towards the stone throwers meaningfully, menacingly, whip in hand, and they soon ran off.

But some were more determined than others, and came back with their dogs to unsettle the herd and scatter the sheep. In the confusion – if they could, while Goodlad and I were distracted trying to gather them all in again and drive them on – they'd try to steal away a sheep or a cow. We lost more than a few that way. Drover Morgan helped us chase the strangers away, round up the herd and the flock again, but he never blamed us.

'That's people,' he'd say. 'There's some that give and some that take. We're bound to lose one or two. It happens. Not to worry.'

But he did worry when Goodlad came back wounded after we'd seen off a pack of village dogs that had attacked us one day. It was my first fight. I did what I could, but they were all stronger than me, faster too. I learnt one thing that day, that I might be small, with little legs, but I could bite just as well as any dog, whatever their size. When we'd finally chased them off, I felt good. I had stood my ground fighting alongside Goodlad. We had saved each other.

I didn't see how it had happened, but once we'd

driven them away Goodlad came back limping, his leg bleeding. Drover Morgan looked after his leg, cleaned it, bandaged it. And for a couple of days Goodlad rode up in front of Drover Morgan on his saddle, and I was left to drive the animals

alone while he recovered. Doing that on my own, I think I must have grown up a year in those two days. From then on, I felt like a proper drover's dog.

We met up more and more now with other drovers and their animals on their way to London markets, just as we were. Of course, Drover Morgan knew them all, and they all knew him. But meeting drovers and their animals didn't make life easy, because the herds and flocks could so easily get mixed up. Every drover had marked his own animals, but picking them out when they got muddled up was a skill I had not mastered.

Luckily Goodlad's leg healed well and quickly so he was there to show me how it was done. The trick was to keep the herds and flocks, and their drover's dogs, as far from each other as possible.

So that's what we tried to do, not always successfully. One or two would always wander off and join other herds or flocks where they didn't belong, but everyone helped everyone else and none went missing. It was just more work, more running about, more growling and barking.

But it was fun too. I liked a little chaos. It was what we were there for, to sort it out. I could see Goodlad was loving it too. He was still limping, but after a few days it didn't seem to bother him that much any more. We charged about, driving the animals on, gathering in strays, tongues hanging out happily, enjoying it, until we'd driven every sheep and cow back where they belonged.

We were all on our own again one warm

evening as we approached a long, wide village green. There was a church with a tall tower, and houses big and small on either side of the green, and there was a pond at the far end outside the village inn. To arrive in such a place after a hard day was always a relief. To find a place with no other drovers and their herds or flocks, where we could rest and eat in peace, was always wonderful.

'Frampton,' Drover Morgan called out to us. 'Best place to stop, isn't it, Goodlad? Nice folk, good beer, all the grass the sheep and cows can eat, all the water they can drink. Perfect.'

We were just coming past the church, heading for the pond ahead of us, when the church bells suddenly began to ring out. The clanging was loud enough to set the birds flying

up in sudden flurries out of the trees. The sheep

took fright and bolted. Down the village green

they went, the cattle stampeding after them,

bellowing in their alarm, kicking up their legs

and tossing their horns as they ran, till they all

reached the pond, where thankfully once one

had stopped they all stopped, remembered how thirsty they were after a long day of walking in the heat. They calmed down and began to drink. If that pond hadn't been there, I think they'd have gone on stampeding forever.

Everyone came running out of their houses, laughing and hugging each other, dancing, singing. The church bells were still ringing. We had never had a welcome like it. But, strangely, no one seemed to be paying us much attention at all. No children came up to cuddle me. Drover Morgan looked as surprised as we were. He rode over to talk to some of the villagers, who were dancing around, in a circle, arms linked.

'What's up?' he asked them. 'What's all the excitement about?'

'Waterloo!' one of them shouted back. 'We've

beaten Boney at Waterloo! There was a big battle at Waterloo – that's in Belgium or somewhere – and we won. It'll be the end of Napoleon. Boney's a prisoner. He's finished. It means peace! Peace! Peace at last. Get down off that horse, Drover, and join us.'

And that's what Drover Morgan did. He looked around, saw all the animals drinking at the pond or grazing the grass on the green. He looked down at us, a great smile on his face, tears running down his cheeks.

'Can you believe it, boys?' he said. 'Peace! Peace at last! Ring out, sweet bells, ring out!' And then he was linking arms and dancing around with the villagers.

Goodlad and I looked on in amazement. It was wonderful to see everyone so joyously happy, but

we had no idea why. That we would find out later, all about the Battle of Waterloo. I had no idea what a battle was, of course, and had never heard of Waterloo before.

I couldn't know it yet, but it was a battle that would change my life forever. And not just my life, either.

CHAPTER ELEVEN

We stayed in that village for a few days. Drover Morgan said we all needed a good rest – the cattle, the sheep, and especially Goodlad. Goodlad was working as hard as always, but I could see he was slower now when he went after the strays. He was exhausted. He was becoming more and more like a father to me – there at my side when he could be, encouraging me, comforting me when things went wrong, which they did. I'd move too suddenly, too quickly sometimes, and frighten the sheep into bunching too close, or I'd panic the young cattle and set them running. Goodlad was always there to help, to put everything right, calm the animals down, and to reassure me.

I think Drover Morgan decided to rest there at Frampton for a few days mostly because of Goodlad. All of us were tired out, and we had been walking more slowly every day now for a while, and Drover Morgan had often been giving Goodlad a ride up on the horse in front of him. More animals every day were walking lame. My legs hurt with every step, and my feet were feeling tender and sore. For some time, I had been seeking out the soft grass to walk on to protect my feet, avoiding stony tracks and rocks wherever I could.

Frampton was a good place to stop. Drover Morgan was obviously well known and well liked in the village. He must have often passed through with cattle and sheep – everyone knew him. Perhaps it was because of him that no one seemed to mind that our cattle and sheep now grazed on the village green. Goodlad and I kept a good eye on them in case they strayed into the churchyard or into gardens.

The celebrations in the village marking the end of the war with Boney went on day after day. The band played outside the inn. There was much singing and drinking and dancing every evening. And they rang the church bells again and again, loud and long. The animals took no notice now. They were happy wandering the green, grazing, resting, drinking at the pond, chewing the cud contentedly, sleeping under the shade of the trees.

Drover Morgan came out of the inn to bring us our food, and would often sit with us under a great tree on the green, and talk. 'We'll have to be on our way tomorrow, boys,' he said one evening. 'Not far to go to London now. A week, no more, if all goes well. I like it here, but we've got to get these animals to market. Good people, here in this village – kind too, generous-hearted. Not like some.

'Never seen a village so happy. I expect it's like it everywhere all over the country. Nothing like peace after a war. We've been fighting Boney and the Frenchies for twenty years near enough. All over now. Can't believe it. All battles are terrible. But, from what I'm hearing, at Waterloo it was a terrible slaughter. The winners lose. The losers lose. Everyone loses. Don't they realise that? Thousands dead and thousands wounded on both sides. There'll be mothers and fathers and sisters and brothers grieving all over France, all over this country too. And what for? That's what I'd like to know. I mean I've never met a Frenchie, not so far as I know. They'd be much like us, I'm thinking – different language, maybe, different songs, different dances. But they've got families they love like us. They've got sheep and cattle to look after, I expect, like us. We may not agree on this or that. But we could have sat down and made peace before ever a shot was fired.'

He talked to us on and on, long into the night, and then lay down beside us under the tree, the sheep and cattle grunting contentedly all around us. Goodlad had taken to laying his head close to mine when he slept. I was now used to going off to sleep when he did, my breathing in rhythm with his. When he woke, I woke. We were alert together even in our sleep.

Rousing the sheep and cattle in the morning was not easy. Some were unwilling even to get up on their feet. We had to do a lot of running around and barking and nipping at heels before they would be moved. The villagers joined in to help us, whistling and whooping, and then cheering us on our way. And even then the animals walked on only reluctantly, slowly. Maybe they thought they'd arrived, but they hadn't. They were out of the habit, and so was I. My legs were stiff, my feet still sore. Drover Morgan was cracking his whip, whistling us all on. So on we went, on towards London.

However much Drover Morgan had told me, I had little idea, of course, what to expect. Whenever we stopped at an inn for the night, there were more people, and more drovers, with more sheep and cattle. The towns and villages were bigger, the river wider, the buildings often taller. And everywhere we went the people were celebrating the victory at Waterloo. Flags flew, and bells rang out.

Every day there were ever more horses and carts and carriages on the roads. There was just more of everything everywhere, and it was exciting and distracting. Goodlad was there beside me, reminding me not to let my mind wander, that we had a job to do.

And, finally, we did it.

We arrived in the streets of London, and drove our sheep and cows into the chaos and bustle of the market. Keeping our animals apart from the hundreds of others was a nightmare.

We did our best, but I think we lost more of them there in the market when we arrived than during the many long miles of our journey.

Drover Morgan didn't seem to mind that much. He seemed so relieved to have arrived and to have delivered the animals to market, to meet up with other drovers and friends at the inn where we were staying. He fed us well, thanked us again and again for all we'd done. The more beer he drank, the more he thanked us. Goodlad and I slept beside his bed, tired out, happy not to be walking, happy not to be on the move at last. Just happy.

There were other dogs there, some not too friendly. Being small and not the bravest of dogs, I always stayed at Goodlad's side for protection. Any sign of trouble – however big the dog, however fierce he looked – and that growl from deep inside Goodlad was usually enough to warn off any attack. Once or twice, it did come to a fight. It always amazed me when Goodlad transformed himself suddenly from the gentle, kind animal I knew him to be into a fearsome warrior of a dog, hackles raised, lip curled, teeth bared. The fights were always short, the attacker chased away, yelping, tail between his legs.

We stayed a few nights in the inn with Drover Morgan. And then came the surprise.

CHAPTER TWELVE

Drover Morgan was sitting on the bed one morning, scratching his head and yawning away his sleep.

'Well, boys,' he said between his yawns, 'time's come. You've had a few days to rest up. Goodlad knows what happens now. I have to stay in town for a couple of weeks, doing the business, collecting all the money for the farmers. Quite a business, I can tell you. They'd rob you blind up here if they could. Anyway, you two need to go home. Goodlad will show you the way, Cobweb. You just go where he goes. Not difficult. You follow your nose. Go back the same way you came, from inn to inn. The innkeepers all know you're coming. They'll feed you, look after you. All paid for, all arranged, I promise you.'

He bent down, ruffled our heads fondly and patted us. 'You've done well. Been good dogs, best dogs,' he said. Then he was walking to the door and opening it. 'Off you go now, see you back home.'

And that was that. Goodlad didn't hesitate. It was obvious to me then that he was expecting this, that this was what happened at the end of every drive. Off went Goodlad, down the stairs, and I went scuttling after him, out of the inn and into the bustle of the street outside. He looked behind him from time to time to make sure I was following. I was right behind him, dodging my way through the crowd. Lose Goodlad in amongst all these people and I knew I'd never find my way home – never see Bethan again. I kept as close to his swishing tail as I could.

So, walking through those teeming streets of London, I began my long journey home. Goodlad, my guide, my protector and friend, knew the way, and so would be out in front. But if ever he got too far ahead I'd give him a yap to tell him that he should slow down, that I didn't want to be left on my own. In the end, I think he realised I felt happier, safer, walking not behind him at all, but beside him, especially when there were other dogs around, eyeing us from dark alleyways. They were often gathered in packs in the squares, and did not look at all friendly, so whenever we saw them we moved on fast and kept our distance. We kept our eyes down too. There was no point in inviting trouble.

In avoiding these dogs and the carriages and the horses and the crowds, I soon realised we were not following the way we had come with the sheep and cattle. My eyes told me so, my nose told me so. But one glance at Goodlad and I could tell he knew the streets. He seemed very sure of where he was going, so I walked on beside him, reassured.

I was noticing now more and more that London too was still celebrating the victory in this great battle we had already heard about a while ago. There were often bells ringing out, bands playing and more and more soldiers in their uniforms wandering in the streets. They were welcomed everywhere they went with whoops and cheers and hugs. Children would often be marching proudly along beside them, some in soldiers' caps. And as we left London at last we began to see yet more soldiers, on their way home it seemed – in every village or town we passed through, in every inn we stayed at. They sang their songs, and told their stories.

And all the innkeepers were as good as their word. They welcomed us, fed us – some better than others – and gave us shelter for the night before we moved again the next day. We had to be on our guard, though. There were often drover dogs guarding their flocks and herds and we knew we had to be careful not to go anywhere near them. *We* were drover dogs. We knew how fiercely the sheep and cattle had to be protected. A strange dog was always a threat, so we kept well clear.

These soldiers we met, mostly at the inns where we stopped, were not all happy heroes – far from it. And their stories were not all happy stories. Some sat in the inns with tears running down their cheeks, staring silently ahead, cloaked in sadness, their faces grey with it. Many were wounded, bandaged, limping. Some walked on crutches. Some could not walk at all. Many of those were begging in the streets. We saw a few who sat barefoot, begging outside the inns, or by the side of the road, their uniforms ragged and dirty.

One of these wounded soldiers, I noticed, had his head bandaged round his eyes so that he could not see. He had a friend who looked after him all the time, guiding him, their arms linked, and talking to him quietly as they went. This soldier who was guiding him was a giant of a man, his uniform smart, not tattered like so many we had seen. When he looked down at us, I could hear that he was telling his wounded friend all about us, which made his friend smile.

'Dog?' he said. 'What sort of dog? I like dogs.'

'There's two of them, Jonno – one small, funny-looking thing, little legs, big ears, pointy nose. Kind eyes, though. And the other is a collie dog, I think, black and white, but grey round his muzzle, scars on his face. Been in the wars, I reckon. Like us. All on their own they are, Jonno, like us. They been following us for quite a while, or we been following them. Going along together you might say.'

'We had a dog once when we were little, Robbie. You remember Betsy?' said Jonno, the wounded soldier, reaching out his hand to find me. 'Can I touch?'

I felt his fingers feeling along my back up to my neck, then he was stroking me, patting me. No one had touched me so gently since Bethan.

'Better pat the other one too,' said Robbie, the giant of a man, taking Jonno's other hand and guiding it to Goodlad. 'Don't want him feeling left out, do we?' Soon both of them were crouching over us and stroking us, talking to us. They were loving it. We were loving it. 'The collie dog, Jonno, he's got eyes like Betsy,' he said.

'Wish I could see him,' said Jonno. 'Wish I could see them, Robbie. Last thing I saw was that farmhouse at Waterloo, Hougoumont they called it, didn't they? We had to hold it against the Frenchies, didn't we? Lose it and the battle was lost, the officers said. Hold it and the battle was won. Why is it that officers always tell us what we know already, like we're stupid? We all knew that. They knew that too, the Frenchies. And they kept coming, and coming. And we kept shooting and shooting. Brave as lions they were. And that Frenchie drummer boy, Robbie, you remember how he kept coming on? Kept drumming away, till he was standing there all alone. I saw him fall, saw him get up again and come on towards us, shouting to them to follow. *'En avant, camarades! En avant!'* And with all his friends dead all around him. Never forget that. That was a brave lad, bravest I ever saw. And he was the last person I saw, last person I'll ever see.' He was near to tears. I could hear it in his voice.

'You don't know that, Jonno. We'll get you to a doctor soon as we get home. Till then you got me for eyes for a while. You'll share my eyes. I'm your brother, aren't I? One eye each, eh? We'll manage.'

It seemed natural after that for us all to go

on together – chance companions going the same way, easy in one another's company. We found ourselves walking along by a river with the two soldiers all the rest of that day, until we came over a bridge and there ahead of us in a village was the inn we recognised, where we and Drover Morgan and the animals had stayed a while before. There'd be food waiting for us, rest, shelter and the warmth of a fire. How we longed for all of that every evening.

The two soldiers followed us in. What a welcome we all had. Word must have got about when they saw the two soldiers in their uniforms and one of them wounded. Soon the whole village it seemed had followed us and were crowding into the inn to greet us. Jonno, the soldier with the bandaged head, was led to a chair close to us in the inn. He sat down heavily by the fire, exhausted. They ate, we ate, and then the questions started coming, about Waterloo, about the battle. Both were reluctant to talk about it, I could tell.

In the end it was Jonno who answered, his hand resting all the while on my neck, trembling sometimes as he spoke. Everyone listened. Nothing could be heard in that crowded inn but the crackling of the fire, and the occasional log shifting, and the soft voice of Jonno replying. Goodlad and I listened as intently as anyone there, not understanding everything, perhaps, but enough.

Then came Jonno's story – the story that changed all our lives forever.

CHAPTER THIRTEEN

'**R**ing me no more bells,' Jonno began. 'On
account of that battle my eyes will never see
again. On account of that battle many thousands
of us are dead on both sides. The Frenchies
were brave. We were brave. Their families
will be grieving; our families will be grieving.
There's soldiers without seeing eyes now, like

me. There's soldiers without legs, arms. It's like that after a battle. And Waterloo was the biggest, most terrible battle I've ever been in – and Robbie and me, we've been in lots. Been soldiering for ten years. We've won some and lost some. At the end of that battle at Waterloo, our flags were still flying, their eagles lay in the mud. In the end, we came home, some of us. In the end, they went home. Bells for us. No bells for them. We won, they say. They lost, we say. We all lost, I say. So ring me no more bells.

'In inns like this up and down the country, I expect soldiers like us, on our way home, are being welcomed like conquering heroes. You know why we fought, why they fought, why we died, they died? I'll tell you: you fight for your comrade standing next to you, your brother in arms, your uniform, your regiment, your flag, your eagle. Weren't the country, weren't because we hated the Frenchies, weren't because they hated us. We fought because we wanted to live, to survive, to see the faces of everyone we love, the fields and hedgerows where we grew up. See home again.

'I cannot tell you about the whole battle, only our little part in it. There were thousands of them, thousands of us, perhaps more guns gathered together in this battle than ever before on this earth – that's what they say. And horses. Horses and men, we fought together, fell together. It was a great and terrible slaughter. They tell us that we very nearly lost, that we were just about holding out when the Prussian army – our allies against Boney, they were – they arrived on the field at the last moment and saved the day.

'We never saw the Prussians from where we were at the farmhouse at Hougoumont. Coldstream Guards we are, my brother Robbie and me. We had three other pals from the same village – known each other since we were little. They were killed that day. They're never coming home. We Coldstreams had to keep the Frenchies from climbing over the farmhouse walls, overrunning us and

driving us out. Sometimes they came over, and
their tricolour flew high on the walls. But we
drove them out again, and our flag flew again in
the smoke of the battle. The killing was terrible,

the dying too. So ring me no bells.

'That was our battle. But the battle I will remember till the day I die was fought by one boy against a whole army, against us – that

Frenchie drummer boy who was the bravest of the brave. The Frenchies had broken through the gate, led by the drummer boy, who was walking on ahead. He was drumming and shouting through the noise of the battle, all the yelling,

and the musket fire, and the artillery shells, and the screams of the dying. "*En avant*," he was shouting. "*Vive l'empereur! Vive la France. En avant, en avant!*"

'Their charge faltered under our fire. But this drummer boy kept coming, kept drumming. And the Frenchies followed him, cheering as they came on, as they died. We managed to close the gates behind him. Soon that boy was the only one left alive, and still he drummed defiantly, looking up at us, fearlessly. Any one of us could have shot him down. No one did. All of us were in awe of his courage. In the end, my brother, Robbie here, climbed down, and went over to him, towering over him. He saluted him, and the drummer boy saluted him back.'

Jonno turned to his brother, holding out a

hand to him for reassurance. 'He had no weapons,' he went on. 'You tried gently to take his drum, didn't you? But he would not let you have it. I remember the lads were all cheering as you brought the lad in. I saw the look of defiance on his face, changing to bewilderment. And I saw the tears in his eyes. That's all I remember. That's when the shell came over and landed close, too close, and I was in the way of it. And the world about me splintered and went black.' His voice broke then. 'You tell the rest, Robbie. You saw it, you and the lads made it happen.'

His brother took a while to pick up the story. He, like everyone listening, was overcome. 'Well, when it was all over, we were marched away, through the smoke and past the dreadful debris of the battlefield. The Frenchie prisoners we had taken were left behind, under guard. But we kept the drummer boy with us in our ranks as we marched away, the fifes and drums playing.

'We all knew he'd never killed any of us, not with his drum. We all knew the Frenchie prisoners would be heading for some dark prison somewhere in England. None of us wanted this to happen to the drummer boy, not after the courage we had all seen. He was just a boy, anyway – too young to go to prison, and too brave as well. French or not.

'Luck played a part in what happened next. It often does. As we marched away, we saw the officers on their horses come riding past us, surveying the battlefield. I recognised Wellington at once – we all did, and gave him a cheer. Nosey, we called him. He was easy to recognise from his

huge nose and the huge bay horse he was riding,
and the funny hat he always wore.

'I did it on the spur of the moment. I broke
ranks and went over to him. He looked down
at me from high on his horse, smiling suddenly

when he recognised my uniform.

'"Coldstream Guards," he said. "You've stood firm here at Hougoumont. You are the best of us. We should have lost the battle if you had not held this farmhouse. A close-run thing it was. Your face tells me you have something to ask of me. Ask away."

'So I told him all about the heroism of the French drummer boy, who he could see in amongst my comrades behind him. I said that all of us Coldstreams did not want him to end up in a prison, that he deserved better. I asked if we could just let him go home. Nosey asked for him to be brought over. So the great commander and the French drummer boy met. Neither spoke for a while.

'Then Nosey said: "I never thought the

enemy looked like this. Brave boy, brave soldier, French or not. You take him to England. Let him keep his drum. Find him a home if you can. He fought bravely for his emperor, and I fear from the look on his face that he would do so again. So we shan't set him free in France. In England, once the war is over, there will come a time when all that divides us is the Channel, then he may want to become one of us. I like that idea. Yes, take him home, and look after him. You have my blessing."

'So that's what we did. The drummer boy came back home onboard the ship with us. To protect him and to honour him, we gave him the uniform of a Coldstream drummer boy. He never spoke a single word to us, nor to anyone else. He kept his drum always with him, never played it, no matter how often we asked him to. We tried all we could to be friends, but he would not even look at us. He wouldn't even tell us his name. He sat always on his own, ate alone, slept alone. We talked long about what was to be done with him when we arrived home in England.

'It was Jonno's idea. "We'll bring him home to our village, Robbie. It'll take a while, but he'll learn to speak English, become one of us. Some won't like it, some won't ever like a Frenchie, and you can't blame them. By the look of him, he doesn't like us much, does he? Give him time, give them time, give us all time."

'And it was true: some of the soldiers onboard did not like having him there, and made no secret of it. They glared at him darkly as they passed by, but none dared say anything or do anything. They knew they'd have to answer to

Jonno and me if they did.

'When we disembarked at Tilbury, the drummer boy was with us one moment and gone the next. Vanished into nowhere. We went looking for him in the streets all around, and one of us found his uniform tunic, hanging on a tree down by the river. But of him and of his drum there was no sign. Lord knows where he is. Found a boat and gone back home to France, to his family, I shouldn't wonder, if he can get there. Good luck to him, I say. All of us soldiers, us lot, their lot, my pal here and me, it's all a soldier wants, to go home, at last, back where we belong.'

I understood those words so well. Soldiers, dogs, no matter who we are, we all want to go home, be back where we belong. And I belonged back on the farm with my Bethan.

CHAPTER FOURTEEN

Goodlad and I, we walked along with the two soldiers for several days after that, stopped at the same inns. I'm not sure who was following who. We liked their company, and they seemed to like ours. We basked in the welcome they received wherever we went. Everyone seemed to assume the four of us were together. And in a way we were. They told their story of the battle and of the Frenchie drummer boy, more than once. And always it was Jonno, the blind brother, who told it, and I would sit close to him because I knew he wanted me beside him, to rest his hand on my neck and feel me there. I think I felt closer to him then than to any other human being besides Bethan.

Goodlad, old and stiffer now in his legs, led the way, nose to the ground, nose in the air, scenting his way home. I watched him, following his example, knowing this was how he knew where to go. We came, after many days, to that same village with a long straight green, houses and wide streets and great trees on either side – the village where the church bell had rung out so loud as we passed, where we'd first heard of the Battle of Waterloo, and where the animals had stampeded all through the village till they reached the pond at the end of the green. There was the inn where Drover Morgan had stayed, where we had slept at the bottom of his bed.

Already we had been noticed. The people came running out of their houses to greet the two soldiers. And soon enough the bells were ringing again.

We walked into the inn with our two soldiers, and this landlord knew at once who we were.

'You know these two dogs?' Robbie asked him.

'Course we do. The collie one specially. He's been here often, haven't you, my son? And last time this one with the little legs was with him. They was here passing through a few weeks back.

Drover dogs they are, Drover Morgan's dogs, on their way home to Wales.'

'Wales? That's hundreds of miles away, isn't it?' said Jonno. 'How do they find their way?'

'Who knows?' replied the landlord. 'Like a swallow does, like a salmon does. They know the way home, don't they? Reckon they know, but they're not saying! Intelligent, that's what those drover dogs are. Understand a lot more than we think they do.'

That evening the whole village gathered there in the inn to greet the two soldiers. Goodlad and I stayed close to them throughout the celebrations. They made a great fuss of us. They sang, they danced, they laughed, and cried too. And then came the questions about the battle.

'Did you see the emperor – did you see

Boney? Did the Frenchies run away?'

'No, never saw Boney,' said Robbie. 'And no, the Frenchies never ran away. We wished they would, but they never did. They stood and they fought. Fine soldiers, make no mistake. Bravest soldier we ever saw was a Frenchie drummer boy.'

And they'd tell the drummer boy story again and, as always, everyone there listened in the deepest silence.

We watched them all afterwards, drifting away from the inn, to their homes across the green, quietened by the story, as always happened.

The next day we set off, following Goodlad as usual. It was afternoon when we came to the crossroads that was to be the parting of our ways.

'We go north from here, up to our home

in the Borders,' said Robbie. 'To Scotland, to Dumfries. And you, we now know, must go west into Wales. Don't have to tell you the way, do we? We shall miss you. But we shall remember you.

Be safe, my friends – go safe.' He crouched down, patted us, pulled our ears fondly as he did, and then stood up to go.

That was the last we saw of our friends.

There are many times in my life I have wished I could speak as people speak. This was one of them. I was standing now close to Jonno's leg, so he could feel I was there. He crouched down and buried his face in my neck.

'Thank you, Cobweb,' he said. 'That landlord last night told me your name. I shan't ever forget you. Go well, boy, go well.'

We watched them walk away till they were out of sight.

It felt suddenly lonely out on the road, with just the two of us. Until now the weather had been kind to us, but we were up in the hills and walking into a cold mountain wind. And with the wind came a driving rain. There was nowhere to shelter up there. We knew we had to keep going. We had no choice. When the rain stopped at long last, we found ourselves in thick fog. Now more than ever I needed Goodlad to guide me. I was following him as closely as I could. But more than once, as the evening came on, I lost sight of him in the gloom. And then I had to rely on my own instinct, my own nose. It was the hardest day of our journey. There seemed no end to it. We were both cold, shivering with it, and exhausted.

We heard sheep bleating ahead of us in the fog, and then we were suddenly in amongst them, and there were white shadows all around us, scattering in panic. There was angry barking and shouting. We ran. We lost all sense of where we were going. It didn't matter any more. Escape was all that mattered. We ran on, downhill now, slipping and sliding and stumbling over the scree. On and on we went till the barking stopped and there was no more shouting and no more bleating.

We came to a stream too deep and fast to cross, and walked along it until we reached a bridge. Through the gloom on the other side, we could see there were houses ahead. We had no idea where we were. Goodlad had his nose to the ground trying to pick up the trail. I was doing the same. There was no trail. We were lost. We wandered into a village, still hoping against hope it was one we might recognise. One look between us and we both knew we had never been here before.

The village looked almost deserted. There were one or two lighted windows, smoke rising from a few chimneys, a looming church tower and a wide road running through. But no people.

But then we saw an inn ahead, beyond the church, and we heard voices inside. We came closer – felt the warmth from inside, smelt food. Goodlad was hesitating. This was not an inn he recognised and neither did I. But we were cold to the bone, wet through and tired. We needed shelter and warmth and food. We needed them badly. We found a woodshed behind the inn, crawled in amongst the logs, lay there and waited. At least we had shelter now. But that was all we had.

And then lying there half asleep in the darkness we heard something strange, a pulsating sound in amongst the murmur of voices from the inn. Curious, we crept out of our shed, and through the back door of the inn. There standing by the window, surrounded by a crowd of listeners, was a drummer boy, beating his drum, all eyes and ears on him. And when he had finished they all burst into applause. He started up again, a new more spirited rhythm, and soon had everyone clapping along in time.

We walked in and lay down by the fire, quite unnoticed until the drummer boy saw us lying there. I could see at once he knew we were watching him. I thought he almost smiled, as if he was pleased to see us. Looking straight at us, he went on drumming, the rattling and the tapping ever faster, faster, the thundering louder, louder.

By the time he finished, everyone was banging the tables, and whooping and cheering, and some were dropping coins into his hat as they left. That was when we heard him speak for the first time.

He was punching the air in triumph. 'Waterloo! Waterloo!' he cried. 'I was there!'

CHAPTER FIFTEEN

When everyone had left, the drummer boy picked up his drum and beckoned us over to him. We followed him up the stairs into a bedroom, where he threw himself down on the bed, and patted it, inviting us to jump up.

He spoke softly, almost in a whisper. '*Vous savez*, they feed me wherever I go,' he said.

'All I say is, "Waterloo, I was there." And I am a hero. I learn this very quickly. And then I do my drumming. They can see it is a French drum. I say I captured it at Waterloo. And they look after me like I am the emperor or the king. I speak English – but only a little, because I do not want them to hear my French accent. I learn it in the army with English prisoners of war. Drummer boys, we have to do everything in the Grande Armée, not just play drums. We are also messengers on the battlefield.

'Once I bring a message from Marshal Ney to the emperor, to Napoleon. I talk to him. He talk to me. *C'est vrai*. He ask me where I live. "On a farm in Brittany, sire," I tell him. He ask me my name. "Patrick Bounine," I say to him.

'And you know what he say? *"Bonjour,*

Patrick. *Je suis Napoleon Bonaparte*." And he rode away.

'And sometimes we drummers have to carry food and water to soldiers, and often also to English prisoners of war. These prisoners, they talk to me and I listen and I learn. So I speak some English, maybe more than you.' He laughed. 'You are alone now, I think. Those two soldiers I saw with you are not with you any more, are they? I saw you walking with them. They were kind to me. I will speak to you always in English, to practise, *vous comprenez*. I must sound like I am English. I must practise.' He sat up and looked at us closely. '*Vous désirez manger?* Your eyes and your tongues tell me you want food. I will find some.'

He left the room, and a while later came back

carrying a plate of sausage and cheese. 'Anything I want, I told you. I was a drummer at the Battle of Waterloo. I do not say which side. They give me anything I want. I play my drum and they put money in my hat.'

We ate ravenously off the plate, and when we had finished we jumped on the bed again to be with him. We were busy licking ourselves clean after our meal, when he began to talk to us, quietly – almost in a whisper.

'You are the only ones who know my secret,' he began. 'You know I am Patrick Bounine, drummer in the Grande Armée. I have another secret to tell you. At Waterloo I was not brave. I was lucky. My *maman* told me when I went away to war that luck would always be kind to me. She was wrong. We lost the Battle of Waterloo, so fate was not kind. But my life was saved that day at Hougoumont. So she was right also.

'Everyone says I was brave that day. *Pas vrai.* Only a few days before the battle I heard news that my *maman* was dead. My older brother, André, he was killed in Russia three years ago. *Une grande tristesse.* It was such sadness. Maman died from this sadness. It was not courage that made me keep drumming that day, that kept me walking on and on, drumming on and on, towards the British guns. I did not care if I died. The truth is I had nothing to live for. So I am not the brave drummer boy they all think I am.'

For some time, he could not bring himself to speak.

'*Alors, mes amis,*' he went on, 'I have no family in France, no friends, no home to go back to. Most of my friends died at Waterloo in that last charge against the walls at Hougoumont. In all the world, I have only this drum, and you two.'

He looked at us, his eyes smiling now through his tears. '*Non*, I think Maman was right. Maybe fate is kind to me after all. It is luck we met before, and luck that we meet again here. I think it was meant to happen. Maybe you are my family now.' He looked at Goodlad and I and said softly, 'Where you go, I will go. Where I go, you will go.'

The next morning, we left early, before anyone in the village was up and about. Of the three of us, only Goodlad had any idea where we were going. Patrick followed where he led, and so did I. I could not work out how he knew the way. It did occur to me after a while that there might be more than one way home, that Drover Morgan might have come on this path with Goodlad and the sheep and cattle at some time back in the past, and that Goodlad was remembering. I never once doubted that one way or another he would find the way, somehow.

At every town and village we came to, Patrick began to drum, so the people soon knew we were there. And, sooner or later, he'd be calling out. 'Waterloo! Waterloo! I was there! I was there!' He'd stop by the marketplace, or in the village square, drop his cap at his feet and drum away. A crowd would soon gather, so there were always enough coins in his cap by the end of the day. He never went hungry. We never went hungry.

Sometimes the town band would come and play with him. Goodlad and I sat beside him as he drummed. And Goodlad would often close his eyes and go off to sleep. The walking tired him these days more and more. Luckily for both of us, we always found some shelter for the night wherever we were. Patrick's drumming, and any mention of Waterloo, of course, usually ensured the warmest of welcomes, opened doors and warmed hearts. Patrick was always offered food and a bed each night. And we two were quite happy curled up at the end of it, fed and watered. All was well.

But not always.

It was all going so well the morning when it happened. We were down in a green valley, walking through meadows along a river bank, and Goodlad suddenly stopped, and lifted his nose to sniff the wind. At once he was off, splashing down into a shallow river, barking excitedly and setting the ducks flying. I loved doing that. They make even more noise than crows if you surprise them. I followed him, as did Patrick, wading through the river, holding his drum above his head.

Goodlad was running now, faster than I'd seen him move for a long while. He reached the top of the hill, sniffed the ground, barking excitedly as if he was after rabbits. Then he stood there waiting for us to join him, his tail straight out behind him, his nose pointing. I sniffed too, looked about me to be sure. Then I knew. Goodlad had found the trail – found the path home the way we had come. I chased him about, barking my head off, telling him just how clever he was.

Patrick, of course, had no idea what the fuss was all about. But when we set off again at speed down the hill he knew he had to follow us.

It was in the next village we came to that it all went wrong. I recognised it, so did Goodlad – the inn where we had stayed with Drover Morgan, the green where the animals had grazed, the stream where they had watered. But somehow the green wasn't the same, not at all as I remembered it. There were hundreds of people milling about – there was music playing, tents and stalls. And there were dogs, several dogs, who were already giving us the eye as we approached. They were gathering together in a pack. Beside me, Goodlad's hackles went up, and the growl was already in his throat. I imitated him. But our warning was not working.

The pack was coming towards us now down the village street, heads lowered, howling. Then they were coming for us, charging, attacking.

CHAPTER SIXTEEN

I would have turned and run, run for my life. But Goodlad stood calmly on one side of me, stood where he was, just eyeing them, and Patrick was on the other. Neither was flinching. They were not running, so I would not run. They moved closer to me, and the three of us stood there waiting for the onslaught, ready for a fight, and knowing we did not stand a chance.

By this time, the crowd of people on the green had seen what was happening. A few were chasing after the dogs, calling them back, but most just stood there, cheering them on.

With every moment, the pack was coming nearer, their barking and baying and snarling louder all the time. They were close enough now for us to see their teeth, and the fury in their eyes. Still we stood, waiting for the worst. That was the moment I heard the drumming start up. Patrick was walking steadily towards them, drumming away, yelling his defiance, our defiance. And we walked with him, the beating of the drum filling me with courage.

The pack was hesitating, slowing, puzzled, alarmed, and then terrified as we came on after them to the sound of the drum. They turned and ran, yelping now, not snarling any more, tails between their legs. Patrick did not stop his drumming till the pack had scattered, until all the dogs had disappeared, the bravest of them hiding

now behind the trousers of their masters or the skirts of their mistresses.

As the dogs vanished, so the children appeared, running towards us, towards the drumming, some marching and skipping along with the drumming.

'Waterloo! Waterloo! I was there! I was there!' Patrick called out again and again as we came through the crowd. And now the people were clapping, cheering us on, giving us as warm a welcome as we'd ever had anywhere.

I was not quite sure what we'd walked into at first that day. I have been to many a country fair since, where people come from far and wide, where there is music and dancing and stalls selling all manner of things, from clogs to blankets, from pies to potatoes. What no one expected that day was a drummer boy from the Battle of Waterloo with two of Drover Morgan's dogs.

Patrick hardly ever spoke to anyone – I had noticed that. He would talk to us all the time when we were alone together, but was always more nervous when strangers were around. And when he did speak amongst strangers it was with one-word answers.

'Where are you going?' was the question they most often asked him.

'Home,' he would say. Nothing more.

Patrick let his drum do his talking. Everyone wanted to hear him drumming. The children wanted to march along with him wherever he went, to try drumming on his drum themselves. He loved to show them. At the inn that evening, Goodlad and I were welcomed in and looked after by the innkeeper – an old friend of Drover Morgan – and of course many in the village recognised us from the time some weeks before when we'd passed through with Drover Morgan and all the sheep and cattle, and spent the night there at the inn.

We were about to set off early the next morning when we were approached from across the road by a young man, who was walking with some difficulty on a crutch. I had noticed him the day before at the fair. Many of the children followed us everywhere we went, begging Patrick to play his drum again or to let them have a turn. I remembered this young man being there too, just watching us from a distance. Now he came up to us. I could tell he had something on his mind that was troubling him – something he had to tell Patrick.

His words came out slowly, hesitantly. 'I think I know you,' he said. 'I remember you. You are French. Waterloo. I was there. I was there too. At Hougoumont, at the farmhouse. I fought with the Coldstream Guards. I was on the walls when you and the French infantry came bursting through the gates. We were waiting for you, rifles at the ready. You were the first through the gates, drumming. I saw your friends fall all around you. And you came on, walking through the hail of bullets, drumming, drumming. We could not believe it. We never saw such courage. When we took you prisoner, I shook your hand. Many of us did. Then later I was on the boat with you, coming back to England, with the Coldstreams – those of us that were left. What you are doing here, wandering the countryside with your drum and these dogs I do not know, and I do not care. Your secret is safe with me. The war is over. We were enemies at Waterloo, but friends now.' He held out his hand. 'I wish you well, my friend. *Bonne chance*. Good luck.'

Patrick did not take his hand. Instead, he reached up and put his hands on the man's shoulders, and kissed him on both cheeks. '*Merci, monsieur*,' he said. And sometime later, as we were walking away out of the village, he said, 'I think you understand everything, you two. You do not need words, French or English. *Si j'ai bien compris* – if I have understood well, you know your way home. My drum and I, we shall stay with you until you are safely home. *On y va, mes amis*. To your home, wherever it is.'

CHAPTER SEVENTEEN

Sometimes Goodlad led the way, and sometimes it was me. As the days passed, I found I knew the way almost as well as he did. It wasn't just my nose and my eyes and my memory that were guiding me. It was all of them, but it was instinct more than anything that was pointing the way, and I followed where it led.

With each day now, I could feel we were closer to home. Goodlad I could see was tiring more and more, and was letting me lead most of the way. He would walk on behind with Patrick. How Patrick knew, I could never understand, but whenever I needed it – when I was tiring, and cold and miserable, when it felt as if we would never get there – the drumming would start up from behind me, urging me on. Nothing could have raised my spirits more. He drummed us up to the top of hill after hill, through storm after storm, and to celebrate our arrival, or so it felt to me, he drummed us into every town or village. And, of course, out would come the people and the children, to welcome us.

'Waterloo! Waterloo!' Patrick would call out. 'I was there! I was there!' And someone would recognise Goodlad as Drover Morgan's dog, and soon one of the children would remember me as the drover dog with the little legs they had cuddled only a few weeks before as we passed through with our sheep and cattle. Without exception there was a place for us at every inn that we had stayed at before with Drover Morgan. And without exception – although sometimes local dogs were less friendly – we drover dogs were made more than welcome, and Patrick, of course, was always treated with great honour and affection, as the conquering hero of Waterloo returning home.

With every day now, I could feel the sea was closer. The light in the sky ahead of us was different, brighter, clearer. The sea wind that I remembered so well was whipping around us, chilling us to the bone as we walked. But I did not mind. We were nearly there, nearly home. I could smell the sea on the air. The trees in the hedgerows told me we could not be far away now. Every one we saw was small and stunted, all bent the same way, reminding me of the trees on Bethan's farm. And the houses we passed, like the trees, were low and stunted too, and built like the farmhouse where my Bethan lived.

In those very last days of our long trek home, Goodlad took up the lead. I could see that, like me, he longed to be home at last, to rest. He was struggling on the hills, and often too exhausted even to eat when we arrived at the next village. He drank and he slept – it was all he could do. But he was always up the next morning, and raring to go. It was Patrick's drumming that kept him going, kept him walking on, kept me going, kept me walking on too.

During the whole journey, Goodlad and I had never argued or disagreed about anything. I went where he went. He went where I went. We fed alongside one another, leaving plenty for each other. We had worked the animals together, shared the work, shared everything. But right at the end of our journey we stood on a hill and argued. He wanted to go one way. I wanted to go the other.

From the top of the hill I could see the sea at last – see Bethan's farm, and the barns and the fields all around, and there was Treasure Island beyond. I was home. Except that I wasn't yet. Goodlad wanted to go another way, down into the valley towards another farm, Drover Morgan's

farm, to which I had been taken so long ago, where

I had been tied up, and been so miserable at being

taken away from Bethan. It was Goodlad's home,

not mine. He could go there if he liked and wait

for Drover Morgan to come back, but I was going

home to Bethan and nothing was going to stop

me. We stood there barking at one another on the top of that hill, both of us as determined as the other to have our way.

In the end it was Patrick who decided for us. '*Alors, mes amis.* I see the sea. In France, in Brittany, I live by the sea. I love the sea. You can stand here and argue if you like. I am going to see the sea.' And off he went, leading us for the first time, drumming his way towards the sea, Goodlad and I following on.

He drummed us all the way there. And all the way there I could see Treasure Island ahead of us, the shining sea all around, beckoning me on. I was coming home, coming home!

And that was when I remembered *how* I had left home – how that woman had taken me away, swinging in the darkness of the sack, and how she would still be there. I hadn't forgotten her, but I suppose I'd put her out of my mind for so long. So, much as I was longing to see Bethan, I also had a sudden dread in my heart as we walked up the lane into the farmyard.

There were cattle in the field by the house, and smoke rose from the chimney. I barked and

I barked, but no one came. I ran into the barn. It was empty. I searched in every shed and stable. Empty. When I came back out, Patrick was making his way down the track to the sea, Goodlad at his heels. I ran after them, following them down the cliff path to the sea.

The boat was coming in, Bethan rowing, her back to us, Tad sitting there with a sheep in his arms.

I ran out on to the beach, barking, barking.

Bethan turned and saw me.

She didn't seem to believe her eyes at first. Tad was just sitting there, gaping at me.

'Cobweb! Cobweb!' Bethan was up on her feet, the boat drifting in over the shallows, one oar in the water. As she leapt out and came splashing towards me, I was already in the water.

She caught me up in her arms and hugged me and hugged me.

Patrick had put down his drum, and went wading into the water to pull in the boat, and to help Tad out with the sheep. Tad looked at him, looked at me, and looked at Goodlad. 'That's Drover Morgan's dog, isn't it? That's Goodlad. But where's Drover Morgan? And you, young man, with that drum, who are you?'

CHAPTER EIGHTEEN

As for me, I was being hugged by my Bethan, her face buried in my neck, shaking with her crying, then holding me up in front of her so that we were face to face, nose to nose. 'Where have you been, Cobweb? What did they do with you? She kidnapped you. We didn't know. We came back from the island that evening, Tad and me, and you were gone. She said you'd run off. We looked for you everywhere, called for you, asked everyone round about if anyone had seen you.

'I didn't believe her, and neither did Tad. You would never have just run off and not come back. We both knew that. In the end, I got it out of her, how she hated you and me too, and how she wanted you out of the house and off the farm, how we'd never see you again. And you know what Tad did? He said she had no right to have done what she did. He packed her bags, and drove her into town. We haven't seen her since. Oh, Cobweb, I've missed you – missed you so much.'

It was the best news. Bethan only had to speak of her, and it was as if I could feel Megan's fingers digging into me like claws as she'd carried me off that day. I could hear the hiss of hate in her voice. And now she was gone – the woman in the bonnet was gone.

Until then, Bethan had hardly noticed Patrick standing there, still holding the sheep and looking rather puzzled, Goodlad beside him. Tad had walked over to the drum and was looking down at it, then at Goodlad, then at me.

'I thought so,' he said. 'That's definitely Goodlad. Megan must've handed Cobweb over to Drover. The two of them, they've been off droving, and the two dogs have come home on their own, as they do. They've come back together. I told you, Bethan. Remember, I told you that could be where she might have taken Cobweb to get rid of him. And you said she'd dropped him down a well like as not. She was bad, that woman, wicked to do what she did, but not that wicked.'

Then he bent down and picked up the drum. 'Yours, young man?' Tad asked, examining it.

'Waterloo,' said Patrick. 'I was there.'

'Bit young to go for a soldier, aren't you?'

'Fifteen,' Patrick told him. 'Drummer boy.'

'And you was in the battle?' Tad said. 'You was there? You see Wellington?' Patrick nodded, reaching out and taking his drum back. 'You see Boney, Napoleon?' Patrick nodded again and said nothing. 'Don't say much, do you?'

'Tad!' Bethan said. 'Stop it. Leave him be. He's fought at Waterloo. He's brought Cobweb home. A hero twice over. We got to be kind to him, look after him, just like he must have looked after

Cobweb.' Then she was speaking to Patrick. 'I'm fifteen too,' she said, smiling at him. 'Will you play it – play the drum for us?'

It was a strange procession coming up the track
from the beach, up through the fields towards the
farmhouse – Goodlad and me rummaging through

the bracken, dashing up the paths, barking at the crows; Bethan chasing after us, the sheep bleating after her; Patrick beating on the drum; and Tad coming along behind, leaning heavily on his stick. When I reached the yard, I barked for Mother, and out she came from the barn, not alone, but with a whole new family of puppies all around her, yapping at her. She ran over to me. We nuzzled and licked one another as long as we could before the new family arrived to claim her back.

I stood with Goodlad in the farmyard and barked and barked, while Patrick drummed and drummed. I had never been so happy. I was home, and everyone I loved was there with me.

We filled the kitchen that evening, ate and

drank our fill, then Goodlad and I lay down close to the fire, and slipped into a contented sleep. I woke when Bethan picked me up and settled me down on her lap.

'If only you could talk, Cobweb,' she said. 'You could tell us all your adventures – where you've been, who you've met, everything.'

'Patrick could tell us a thing or two about the battle, about Waterloo, couldn't you?' said Tad, who had hardly spoken all evening. 'But I'm not sure he wants to.'

'Why do you say that, Tad?' Bethan asked. 'Maybe he's shy – that's all. Leave him be.'

'It's his drum that's bothering me. It's a Frenchie drum. Not one of ours, no regimental colours. You can see the colours of the French flag all round the rim. Have a look. Red, white and blue. See? And another thing. He doesn't talk much, does he? And when he does, he speaks funny-like. I put two and two together. Thing is, I reckon I know who he is. I think I read about him in the newspaper a while back. About a French drummer boy our boys captured in the battle. The bravest of the brave, the newspaper called him. Seems like our boys admired him so much they brought him home to England, almost like they adopted him. And then he just took off – disappeared. That's what the newspaper said. You got anything to say for yourself, young man?'

Patrick did not answer for some time. Then he said: '*Peut-être* . . . it is time to tell truth. I am not brave. At Waterloo, I just kept walking, kept drumming. The brave ones died all around me. Yes, after the battle I have been brought to England, by the Coldstream Guards who we were fighting at Hougoumont, and I ran off. I have been pretending to be English. It is not easy. I try not to speak too much English. I say to everyone, yes, the drum is French, that I found the drum after the battle. Yes, *monsieur*, I am French. But there is nothing for me in France any more. My mother is dead, my brother killed in Russia in the Grande Armée. My family is all gone. These two dogs are all the family I have now in all the world. I have no home.'

'Yes, you have,' said Bethan. 'You brought my Cobweb home to me. This is your family now. This is your home. We don't mind at all – do we, Tad? – if you do not speak English like an Englishman. Because we are Welsh. Tad, Patrick could work with us on the farm. You're always saying how we can't run this farm, look after the sheep and the cows, for much longer with just the two of us, not with you getting older like you are.'

'I grew up on a farm, *en* Bretagne, by the sea,' said Patrick. 'If I could help . . .'

'By the sea?' said Tad. 'Can you handle a boat? Have you been fishing?'

'Since I was little. *Homard* . . . lobster, crab. Here you have rocks like in Bretagne, islands too. The sea is blue sometimes, grey mostly, I think. It is like Bretagne, except you all speak English.'

So Patrick stayed with us in the farmhouse and became one of the family. Goodlad went back shortly afterwards to live with Drover Morgan, and I had a new family to play with. As he aged, Tad did only the work with the cows close to the farmhouse, so he didn't have to walk so far, and Patrick and my Bethan went out fishing together, and, with me, looked after the sheep out on Treasure Island.

Everyone all around knew soon enough that we had the famous French drummer boy from the Battle of Waterloo living and working on the farm, and it wasn't long before they were treating him like he'd always been there. To begin with, there were a few in town, in the market, who wouldn't speak to him, but that didn't last for long. It mattered less and less, as time passed, which side he had been on. He was a Frenchie, but they respected and admired his courage, and soon got to like him as much as we did.

And my days as a drover's dog were not over. Drover Morgan and Goodlad came over

to see us on the farm from time to time. And I
loved to see them. Goodlad and I would go off
on a wander together, just the two of us, my best
friend on four legs.

We came back one day from one of our wanders to discover that Tad and Drover Morgan had worked out a plan. Bethan explained it to us.

'Now you don't have to do this, either of you,' she began. 'To be honest with you, Patrick and me, we're not sure it's a good idea. But Tad and Drover Morgan here want you and Patrick to go droving again with him, just once a year, Cobweb. And he wants you, Goodlad, to stay here with us on the farm and help look after the sheep whilst they're gone. Patrick says he'll do it if you'll do it. I said it's up to you. What do you say, Cobweb?'

Well, of course we went. Patrick liked an adventure, so did I. So, once a year after that, we two went off droving hundreds of sheep and cattle to London with Drover Morgan, and found our way home again on our own as I had before,

Patrick following wherever I led him. He had no sense of direction. I loved being with him, but, as it turned out, not as much as my Bethan did.

I would go with Bethan and Patrick out to the island whenever I could. I always loved to go with them, to go exploring, to chase rabbits and rats, and to dig. They were sitting watching me one day after they had finished looking after the sheep, and laughing. They laughed a lot together. I came and sat down beside them, my nose dirty from digging.

'No treasure, then,' Patrick said, brushing off my nose.

'There's other kinds of treasures,' said my Bethan, taking his hand. 'He found you, didn't he?'

So in the end, as the years went by, I had to

share my Bethan with Patrick. But I didn't mind, not that much. When he went off playing his drum, standing up on the high rocks, as he did often – he loved playing that drum – I had her all to myself.

So I was, and so I am, a happy old dog.

SIR MICHAEL MORPURGO is one of Britain's best-loved writers for children. He has written well over 130 books, many of which have been adapted for film, theatre and TV, and won many prizes, including the Smarties Prize, the Blue Peter Book Award and the Whitbread Award. Michael is also the co-founder, with his wife Clare, of the charity Farms for City Children. In 2018, he was knighted for services to literature and charity.